Dutch Fairy Tales For Young Folks

by

William Elliot Griffis

Dutch Fairy Tales For Young Folks
by William Elliot Griffis

ISBN: 978-93-59320-47-2

Published by

DOUBLE 9 BOOKS

2/13-B, Ansari Road
Daryaganj, New Delhi – 110002
info@double9books.com
www.double9books.com
Tel. 011-40042856

ABOUT THE AUTHOR

William Elliot Griffis (September 17, 1843 - February 5, 1928) was a Congregational clergyman, lecturer, and prolific author from the United States. Griffis grew up in Philadelphia, Pennsylvania, the son of a sea captain who eventually became a coal trader. After Robert E. Lee invaded Pennsylvania in 1863, he served as a corporal in Company H of the 44th Pennsylvania Militia for two months. Following the war, he attended Rutgers University in New Brunswick, New Jersey, where he graduated in 1869. Griffis tutored Tar Kusakabe [ja], a young samurai from the province of Echizen (part of present Fukui), in English and Latin at Rutgers. After a year of travel in Europe, he attended the Reformed Church in America seminary in New Brunswick (now known as the New Brunswick Theological Seminary).

CONTENTS

THE ENTANGLED MERMAID

Long ago, in Dutch Fairy Land, there lived a young mermaid who was very proud of her good looks. She was one of a family of mere or lake folks dwelling not far from the sea. Her home was a great pool of water that was half salt and half fresh, for it lay around an island near the mouth of a river. Part of the day, when the sea tides were out, she splashed and played, dived and swam in the soft water of the inland current. When the ocean heaved and the salt water rushed in, the mermaid floated and frolicked and paddled to her heart's content. Her father was a gray-bearded merryman and very proud of his handsome daughter. He owned an island near the river mouth, where the young mermaids held their picnics and parties and received the visits of young merrymen.

Her mother and two aunts were merwomen. All of these were sober folks and attended to the business which occupies all well brought up mermaids and merrymen. This was to keep their pool clean and nice. No frogs, toads or eels were allowed near, but in the work of daily housecleaning, the storks and the mermaids were great friends.

All water-creatures that were not thought to be polite and well behaved were expected to keep away. Even some silly birds, such as loons and plovers and all screaming and fighting creatures with wings, were warned off the premises, because they were not wanted. This family of merry folks liked to have a nice, quiet time by themselves, without any rude folks on legs, or with wings or fins from the outside. Indeed they wished to make their pool a model, for all respectable mermaids and merrymen, for ten leagues around. It was very funny to see the old daddy merman, with a switch made of reeds, shooing off the saucy birds, such as the sandpipers and screeching gulls. For the bullfrogs, too big for the storks to swallow, and for impudent fishes, he had a whip made of seaweed.

Of course, all the mermaids in good society were welcome, but young mermen were allowed to call only once a month, during the week when the moon was full. Then the evenings were usually clear, so that when the party broke up, the mermen could see their way in the moonlight to swim home safely with their mermaid friends. For, there were sea monsters that loved to plague the merefolk, and even threatened to eat them up! The mermaids, dear creatures, had to be escorted home, but they felt safe, for their mermen brothers and daddies were so fierce that, except sharks, even the larger fish, such as porpoises and dolphins were afraid to come near them.

One day daddy and the mother left to visit some relatives near the island of Urk. They were to be gone several days. Meanwhile, their daughter was to have a party, her aunts being the chaperones.

The mermaids usually held their picnics on an island in the midst of the pool. Here they would sit and sun themselves. They talked about the fashions and the prettiest way to dress their hair. Each one had a pocket mirror, but where they kept these, while swimming, no mortal ever found out. They made wreaths of bright colored seaweed, orange and black, blue, gray and red and wore them on their brows like coronets. Or, they twined them, along with sea berries and bubble blossoms, among their tresses. Sometimes they made girdles of the strongest and knotted them around their waists.

Every once in a while they chose a queen of beauty for their ruler. Then each of the others pretended to be a princess. Their games and sports often lasted all day and they were very happy.

Swimming out in the salt water, the mermaids would go in quest of pearls, coral, ambergris and other pretty things. These they would bring to their queen, or with them richly adorn themselves. Thus the Mermaid Queen and her maidens made a court of beauty that was famed wherever mermaids and merrymen lived. They often talked about human maids.

"How funny it must be to wear clothes," said one.

"Are they cold that they have to keep warm?" It was a little chit of a mermaid, whose flippers had hardly begun to grow into hands, that asked this question.

"How can they swim with petticoats on?" asked another.

"My brother heard that real men wear wooden shoes! These must bother them, when on the water, to have their feet floating," said a third, whose name was Silver Scales. "What a pity they don't have flukes like us," and then she looked at her own glistening scaly coat in admiration.

"I can hardly believe it," said a mermaid, that was very proud of her fine figure and slender waist. "Their girls can't be half as pretty as we are."

"Well, I should like to be a real woman for a while, just to try it, and see how it feels to walk on legs," said another, rather demurely, as if afraid the other mermaids might not like her remark.

They didn't. Out sounded a lusty chorus, "No! No! Horrible! What an idea! Who wouldn't be a mermaid?"

"Why, I've heard," cried one, "that real women have to work, wash their husband's clothes, milk cows, dig potatoes, scrub floors and take care of calves. Who would be a woman? Not I"--and her snub nose--since it could not turn up--grew wide at the roots. She was sneering at the idea that a creature in petticoats could ever look lovelier than one in shining scales.

"Besides," said she, "think of their big noses, and I'm told, too, that girls have even to wear hairpins."

At this--the very thought that any one should have to bind up their tresses--there was a shock of disgust with some, while others clapped their hands, partly in envy and partly in glee.

But the funniest things the mermaids heard of were gloves, and they laughed heartily over such things as covers for the fingers. Just for fun, one of the little mermaids used to draw some bag-like seaweed over her hands, to see how such things looked.

One day, while sunning themselves in the grass on the island, one of their number found a bush on which foxgloves grew. Plucking these, she covered each one of her fingers with a red flower. Then, flopping over to the other girls, she held up her gloved hands. Half in fright and half in envy, they heard her story.

After listening, the party was about to break up, when suddenly a young merman splashed into view. The tide was running out and the stream low, so he had had hard work to get through the fresh water of the river and to the island. His eyes dropped salt water, as if he were crying. He looked tired, while puffing and blowing, and he could hardly get his breath. The queen of the mermaids asked him what he meant by coming among her maids at such an hour and in such condition. At this the bashful merman began to blubber. Some of the mergirls put their hands over their mouths to hide their laughing, while they winked at each other and their eyes showed how they enjoyed the fun. To have a merman among them, at that hour, in broad daylight, and crying, was too much for dignity.

"Boo-hoo, boo-hoo," and the merman still wept salt water tears, as he tried to catch his breath. At last, he talked sensibly. He warned the Queen that a party of horrid men, in wooden shoes, with pickaxes, spades and pumps, were coming to drain the swamp and pump out the pool. He had heard that they would make the river a canal and build a dyke that should keep out the ocean.

"Alas! alas!" cried one mermaid, wringing her hands. "Where shall we go when our pool is destroyed? We can't live in the ocean all the time." Then she wept copiously. The salt water tears fell from her great round eyes in big drops.

"Hush!" cried the Queen. "I don't believe the merman's story. He only tells it to frighten us. It's just like him."

In fact, the Queen suspected that the merman's story was all a sham and that he had come among her maids with a set purpose to run off with Silver Scales. She was one of the prettiest mermaids in the company, but very young, vain and frivolous. It was no secret that she and the merman were in love and wanted to get married.

So the Queen, without even thanking him, dismissed the swimming messenger. After dinner, the company broke up and the Queen retired to her cave to take a long nap! She was quite tired after entertaining so much company. Besides, since daddy and mother were away, and there were no beaus to entertain, since it was a dark night and no moon shining on the water, why need she get up early in the morning?

So the Mermaid Queen slept much longer than ever before. Indeed, it was not till near sunset the next day that she awoke. Then, taking her comb and mirror in hand, she started to swim and splash in the pool, in order to smooth out her tresses and get ready for supper.

But oh, what a change from the day before! What was the matter? All around her things looked different. The water had fallen low and the pool was nearly empty. The river, instead of flowing, was as quiet as a pond. Horrors! when she swam forward, what should she see but a dyke and fences! An army of horrid men had come, when she was asleep, and built a dam. They had fenced round the swamp and were actually beginning to dig sluices to drain the land. Some were at work, building a windmill to help in pumping out the water.

The first thing she knew she had bumped her pretty nose against the dam. She thought at once of escaping over the logs and into the sea. When she tried to clamber over the top and get through the fence, her hair got so entangled between the bars that she had to throw away her comb and mirror and try to untangle her tresses. The more she tried, the worse became the tangle. Soon her long hair was all twisted up in the timber. In vain were her struggles to escape. She was ready to die with fright, when she saw four horrid men rush up to seize her. She attempted to waddle away, but her long hair held her to the post and rails. Her modesty was so dreadfully shocked that she fainted away.

When she came to herself, she found she was in a big long tub. A crowd of curious little girls and boys were looking at her, for she was on show as a great curiosity. They were bound to see her and get their money's worth in looking, for they had paid a stiver (two cents) admission to the show. Again, before all these eyes, her modesty was so shocked that she gave one groan, flopped over and died in the tub.

Woe to the poor father and mother at Urk! They came back to find their old home gone. Unable to get into it, they swam out to sea, never stopping till they reached Spitzbergen.

What became of the body of the Mermaid Queen?

Learned men came from Leyden to examine what was now only a specimen, and to see how mermaids were made up. Then her skin was stuffed, and glass eyes put in, where her shining orbs had been. After this, her body was stuffed and mounted in the museum, that is, set up above a glass case and resting upon iron rods. Artists came to Leyden to make pictures of her and no fewer than nine noblemen copied her pretty form and features into their coats of arms. Instead of the Mermaid's Pool is now a cheese farm of fifty cows, a fine house and barn, and a family of pink-cheeked, yellow-haired children who walk and play in wooden shoes.

So this particular mermaid, all because of her entanglement in the fence, was more famous when stuffed than when living, while all her young friends and older relatives were forgotten.

THE BOY WHO WANTED MORE CHEESE

Klaas Van Bommel was a Dutch boy, twelve years old, who lived where cows were plentiful. He was over five feet high, weighed a hundred pounds, and had rosy cheeks. His appetite was always good and his mother declared his stomach had no bottom. His hair was of a color half-way between a carrot and a sweet potato. It was as thick as reeds in a swamp and was cut level, from under one ear to another.

Klaas stood in a pair of timber shoes, that made an awful rattle when he ran fast to catch a rabbit, or scuffed slowly along to school over the brick road of his village. In summer Klaas was dressed in a rough, blue linen blouse. In winter he wore woollen breeches as wide as coffee bags. They were called bell trousers, and in shape were like a couple of cow-bells turned upwards. These were buttoned on to a thick warm jacket. Until he was five years old, Klaas was dressed like his sisters. Then, on his birthday, he had boy's clothes, with two pockets in them, of which he was proud enough.

Klaas was a farmer's boy. He had rye bread and fresh milk for breakfast. At dinner time, beside cheese and bread, he was given a plate heaped with boiled potatoes. Into these he first plunged a fork and then dipped each round, white ball into a bowl of hot melted butter. Very quickly then did potato and butter disappear "down the red lane." At supper, he had bread and skim milk, left after the cream had been taken off, with a saucer, to make butter. Twice a week the children enjoyed a bowl of bonnyclabber or curds, with a little brown sugar sprinkled on the top. But at every meal there was cheese, usually in thin slices, which the boy thought not thick enough. When Klaas went to bed he usually fell asleep as soon as his shock of yellow hair touched the pillow. In summer time he slept till the birds began to sing, at dawn. In winter, when the bed felt warm and Jack Frost was lively, he often heard the cows talking, in their way, before he jumped out of his bag of straw, which served for a mattress. The Van Bommels were not rich, but everything was shining clean.

There was always plenty to eat at the Van Bommels' house. Stacks of rye bread, a yard long and thicker than a man's arm, stood on end in the corner of the cool, stone-lined basement. The loaves of dough were put in the oven once a week. Baking time was a great event at the Van Bommels' and no men-folks were allowed in the kitchen on that day, unless they were called in to help. As for the milk-pails and pans, filled or emptied, scrubbed or set in the sun every day to dry, and the cheeses, piled up in the pantry, they seemed sometimes enough to feed a small army.

But Klaas always wanted more cheese. In other ways, he was a good boy, obedient at home, always ready to work on the cow-farm, and diligent in school. But at the table he never had enough. Sometimes his father laughed and asked him if he had a well, or a cave, under his jacket.

Klaas had three younger sisters, Trintjé, Anneké and Saartjé; which is Dutch for Kate, Annie and Sallie. These, their fond mother, who loved them dearly, called her "orange blossoms"; but when at dinner, Klaas would keep on, dipping his potatoes into the hot butter, while others were all through, his mother would laugh and call him her Buttercup. But always Klaas wanted more cheese. When unusually greedy, she twitted him as a boy "worse than Butter-and-Eggs"; that is, as troublesome as the yellow and white plant, called toad-flax, is to the farmer--very pretty, but nothing but a weed.

One summer's evening, after a good scolding, which he deserved well, Klaas moped and, almost crying, went to bed in bad humor. He had teased each one of his sisters to give him her bit of cheese, and this, added to his own slice, made his stomach feel as heavy as lead.

Klaas's bed was up in the garret. When the house was first built, one of the red tiles of the roof had been taken out and another one, made of glass, was put in its place. In the morning, this gave the boy light to put on his clothes. At night, in fair weather, it supplied air to his room.

A gentle breeze was blowing from the pine woods on the sandy slope, not far away. So Klaas climbed up on the stool to sniff the sweet piny odors. He thought he saw lights dancing under the tree. One beam seemed to approach his roof hole, and coming nearer played round the chimney. Then it passed to and fro in front of him. It seemed to whisper in his ear, as it moved by. It looked very much as if a hundred fire-flies had united their cold light into one lamp. Then Klaas thought that the strange beams bore the shape of a lovely girl, but he only laughed at himself at the idea. Pretty soon, however, he thought the whisper became a voice. Again, he laughed so heartily, that he forgot his moping and the scolding his mother had given him. In fact, his eyes twinkled with delight, when the voice gave this invitation:

"There's plenty of cheese. Come with us."

To make sure of it, the sleepy boy now rubbed his eyes and cocked his ears. Again, the light-bearer spoke to him: "Come."

Could it be? He had heard old people tell of the ladies of the wood, that whispered and warned travellers. In fact, he himself had often seen the "fairies' ring" in the pine woods. To this, the flame-lady was inviting him.

Again and again the moving, cold light circled round the red tile roof, which the moon, then rising and peeping over the chimneys, seemed to turn into silver plates. As the disc rose higher in the sky, he could hardly see the moving light, that had looked like a lady; but the voice, no longer a whisper, as at first, was now even plainer:

"There's plenty of cheese. Come with us."

"I'll see what it is, anyhow," said Klaas, as he drew on his thick woolen stockings and prepared to go down-stairs and out, without waking a soul. At the door he stepped into his wooden shoes. Just then the cat purred and rubbed up against his shins. He jumped, for he was scared; but looking down, for a moment, he saw the two balls of yellow fire in her head and knew what they were. Then he sped to the pine woods and towards the fairy ring.

What an odd sight! At first Klaas thought it was a circle of big fire-flies. Then he saw clearly that there were dozens of pretty creatures, hardly as large as dolls, but as lively as crickets. They were as full of light, as if lamps had wings. Hand in hand, they flitted and danced around the ring of grass, as if this was fun.

Hardly had Klaas got over his first surprise, than of a sudden he felt himself surrounded by the fairies. Some of the strongest among them had left the main party in the circle and come to him. He felt himself pulled by their dainty fingers. One of them, the loveliest of all, whispered in his ear:

"Come, you must dance with us."

Then a dozen of the pretty creatures murmured in chorus:

"Plenty of cheese here. Plenty of cheese here. Come, come!"

Upon this, the heels of Klaas seemed as light as a feather. In a moment, with both hands clasped in those of the fairies, he was dancing in high glee. It was as much fun as if he were at the kermiss, with a row of boys and girls, hand in hand, swinging along the streets, as Dutch maids and youth do, during kermiss week.

Klaas had not time to look hard at the fairies, for he was too full of the fun. He danced and danced, all night and until the sky in the east began to turn, first gray and then rosy. Then he tumbled down, tired out, and fell asleep. His head lay on the inner curve of the fairy ring, with his feet in the centre.

Klaas felt very happy, for he had no sense of being tired, and he did not know he was asleep. He thought his fairy partners, who had danced with him, were now waiting on him to bring him cheeses. With a golden knife, they sliced them off and fed him out of their own hands. How good it tasted! He thought now he could, and would, eat all the cheese he had longed for all his life. There was no mother to scold him, or daddy to shake his finger at him. How delightful!

But by and by, he wanted to stop eating and rest a while. His jaws were tired. His stomach seemed to be loaded with cannon-balls. He gasped for breath.

But the fairies would not let him stop, for Dutch fairies never get tired. Flying out of the sky--from the north, south, east and west--they came, bringing cheeses. These they dropped down around him, until the piles of the round masses threatened first to enclose him as with a wall, and then to overtop him. There were the red balls from Edam, the pink and yellow spheres from Gouda, and the gray loaf-shaped ones from Leyden. Down through the vista of sand, in the pine woods, he looked, and oh, horrors! There were the tallest and strongest of the fairies rolling along the huge, round, flat cheeses from Friesland! Any one of these was as big as a cart wheel, and would feed a regiment. The fairies trundled the heavy discs along, as if they were playing with hoops. They shouted hilariously, as, with a pine stick, they beat them forward like boys at play. Farm cheese, factory cheese, Alkmaar cheese, and, to crown all, cheese from Limburg-- which Klaas never could bear, because of its strong odor. Soon the cakes and balls were heaped so high around him that the boy, as he looked up, felt like a frog in a well. He groaned when he thought the high cheese walls were tottering to fall on him. Then he screamed, but the fairies thought he was making music. They, not being human, do not know how a boy feels.

At last, with a thick slice in one hand and a big hunk in the other, he could eat no more cheese; though the fairies, led by their queen, standing on one side, or hovering over his head, still urged him to take more.

At this moment, while afraid that he would burst, Klaas saw the pile of cheeses, as big as a house, topple over. The heavy mass fell inwards upon him. With a scream of terror, he thought himself crushed as flat as a Friesland cheese.

But he wasn't! Waking up and rubbing his eyes, he saw the red sun rising on the sand-dunes. Birds were singing and the cocks were crowing all around him, in chorus, as if saluting him. Just then also the village clock chimed out the hour. He felt his clothes. They were wet with dew. He sat up to look around. There were no fairies, but in his mouth was a bunch of grass which he had been chewing lustily.

Klaas never would tell the story of his night with the fairies, nor has he yet settled the question whether they left him because the cheese-house of his dream had fallen, or because daylight had come.

THE PRINCESS WITH TWENTY PETTICOATS

Long, long ago, before ever a blue flax-flower bloomed in Holland, and when Dutch mothers wore wolf-skin clothes, there was a little princess, very much beloved by her father, who was a great king, or war chief. She was very pretty and fond of seeing herself. There were no metal mirrors in those days, nor any looking glass. So she went into the woods and before the pools and the deep, quiet watercourses, made reflection of her own lovely face. Of this pleasure she never seemed weary.

Yet sometimes this little princess was very naughty. Then her temper was not nearly so sweet as her face. She would play in the sand and roll around in the woods among the leaves and bushes until her curls were all tangled up. When her nurse combed out her hair with a stone comb--for no other kinds were then known--she would fret and scold and often stamp her foot. When very angry, she called her nurse or governess an "aurochs,"--a big beast like a buffalo. At this, the maid put up her hands to her face. "Me--an aurochs! Horrible!" Then she would feel her forehead to see if horns were growing there.

The nurse--they called her "governess," as the years went on--grew tired of the behavior of the bad young princess. Sometimes she went and told her mother how naughty her daughter was, even to calling her an aurochs. Then the little girl only showed her bad temper worse. She rolled among the leaves all the more and mussed up her ringlets, so that the governess could hardly comb them out smooth again.

It seemed useless to punish the perverse little maid by boxing her ears, pinching her arm, or giving her a good spanking. They even tried to improve her temper by taking away her dinner, but it did no good.

Then the governess and mother went together to her father. When they complained of his daughter to the king, he was much worried. He could fight strong men with his club and spear, and even giants with his sword and battle-axe; but how to correct his little daughter, whom he loved as his own eyes, was too much for him. He had no son and the princess was his only child, and the hopes of the family all rested on her. The king wondered how she would govern his people, after he should die, and she became the queen. Yet he was glad for one thing: that, with all her naughtiness, she was, like her father, always kind to animals. Her pet was a little aurochs calf. Some hunters had killed the mother of the poor little thing in winter time. So the princess kept the creature warm and it fed out of her hand daily.

It was in gloom and with a sad face that the king walked in the woods, thinking how to make a sweet-tempered lady out of his petulant daughter, who was fast growing up to be a tall, fine-looking woman.

Now when the king had been himself a little boy, he was very kind to all living creatures, wild and tame, dumb and with voice--yes, even to the trees in the forest. When a prince, the boy would never let the axe men cut down an oak until they first begged pardon of the fairy that lived in the tree.

There was one big oak, especially, which was near the mansion of his father, the king. It was said that the doctors found little babies in its leafy branches, and brought them to their mothers. The prince-boy took great care of this tree. He was taught by a wise man to cut off the dead limbs, keep off the worms, and warn away all people seeking to break off branches-- even for Yule-tide, which came at our Christmas time.

Once when some hunters had chased a young she-aurochs, with her two calves, into the king's park, the prince, though he was then only a boy, ran out and drove the rough fellows away. Then he sheltered and fed the aurochs family of three, until they were fresh and fat. After this he sent a skilled hunter to imitate the sound of an aurochs mother, to call the aurochs father to the edge of the woods. He then let them all go free, and was happy to see the dumb brutes frisking together.

Now that the boy-prince was grown to be a man and had long been king, and had forgotten all about the incident of his earlier years, he was one day walking in the forest.

Suddenly a gentle breeze arose and the leaves of the old oak tree began first to rustle and then to whisper. Soon the words were clear, and the spirit in the oak said:

"I have seen a thousand years pass by, since I was an acorn planted here. In a few moments I shall die and fall down. Cut my body into staves. Of these make a wooden petticoat, like a barrel, for your daughter. When her temper is bad, let her put it on and wear it until she promises to be good."

The king was sad at the thought of losing the grand old tree, under which he had played as a boy and his fathers before him. His countenance fell.

"Cheer up, my friend," said the oak, "for something better shall follow. When I pass away, you will find on this spot a blue flower growing. Where the forest was shall be fields, on which the sun shines. Then, if your daughter be good, young women shall spin something prettier than wooden petticoats. Watch for the blue flower. Moreover," added the voice of the tree, "that I may not be forgotten, do you take, henceforth, as your family name Ten Eyck" (which, in Dutch, means "at the oak ").

At this moment, a huge aurochs rushed into the wood. Its long hair and shaggy mane were gray with age. The king, thinking the beast would lower his horns and charge at him, drew his sword to fight the mighty brute that seemed to weigh well-nigh a ton.

But the aurochs stopped within ten feet of the king and bellowed; but, in a minute or two, the bellowing changed to a voice and the king heard these good words:

"I die with the oak, for we are brothers, kept under an enchantment for a thousand years, which is to end in a few moments. Neither a tree nor an aurochs can forget your kindness to us, when you were a prince. As soon as our spirits are released, and we both go back to our home in the moon, saw off my right horn and make of it a comb for use on your daughter's curls. It will be smoother than stone."

In a moment a tempest arose, which drove the king for shelter behind some rocks hard by. After a few minutes, the wind ceased and the sky was clear. The king looked and there lay the oak, fallen at full length, and the aurochs lay lifeless beside it.

Just then, the king's woodmen, who were out--thinking their master might be hurt--drew near. He ordered them to take out the right horn of the aurochs and to split up part of the oak for slaves. The next day, they made a wooden petticoat and a horn comb. They were such novelties that nearly every woman in the kingdom came to see them.

After this, the king called himself the Lord of the Land of Ten Eyck, and ever after this was his family name, which all his descendants bore. Whenever the princess showed bad temper, she was forced to wear the wooden petticoat. To have the boys and girls point at her and make fun of her was severe punishment.

But a curious thing took place. It was found that every time the maid combed the hair of the princess she became gentler and more sweet tempered. She often thanked her governess and said she liked to have her curls smoothed with the new comb. She even begged her father to let her own one and have the comb all to herself. It was not long before she surprised her governess and her parents by combing and curling her own hair. In truth, such a wonderful change came over the princess that she did not often have to wear the wooden petticoat, and after a year or two, not at all. So the gossips nearly forgot all about it.

One summer's day, as the princess was walking in the open, sunny space, where the old oak had stood, she saw a blue flower. It seemed as beautiful as it was strange. She plucked it and put it in her hair. When she reached home, her old aunt, who had been in southern lands, declared it to be the flower of the flax.

During that spring, millions of tiny green blades sprang up where the forest had been, and when summer came, the plants were half a yard high. The women learned how to put the stalks in water and rot the coarse, outer fibre of the flax. Then they took the silk-like strands from the inside and spun them on their spinning-wheels. Then they wove them into pretty cloth.

This, when laid out on the grass, under the sunshine, was bleached white. The flax thread was made first into linen, and then into lace.

"Let us name the place Groen-e'-veld" (Green Field), the happy people cried, when they saw how green the earth was where had been the dark forest. So the place was ever after called the Green Field.

Now when the princess saw what pretty clothes the snow white linen made, she invented a new style of dress. The upper garment, or "rok," that is, the one above the waist, she called the "boven rok" and the lower one, beneath the waist, her "beneden rok." In Dutch "boven" means above and "beneden" means beneath. By and by, when, at the looms, more of the beautiful white linen was woven, she had a new petticoat made and put it on. She was so delighted with this one that she wanted more. One after the other, she belted them around her waist, until she had on twenty petticoats at a time. Proud she was of her skirts, even though they made her look like a barrel. When her mother, and maids, and all the women of Groen-é-veld, young and old, saw the princess set the fashion, they all followed. It was not always easy for poor girls, who were to be married, to buy as many as twenty petticoats. But, as it was the fashion, every bride had to obey the rule. It grew to be the custom to have at least twenty; for only this number was thought proper.

So, a new rule, even among the men, grew up. A betrothed young man, or his female relatives assisting him, was accustomed to make a present of one or more petticoats to his sweetheart to increase her wardrobe.

Thus the fashion prevailed and still holds among the women of the coast. Fat or thin, tall or short, they pile on the petticoats and swing their skirts proudly as they walk or go to market, sell their fish, cry "fresh herring" in the streets, or do their knitting at home, or in front of their houses. In some parts of the country, nothing makes a girl so happy as to present her with a new petticoat. It is the fashion to have a figure like a barrel and wear one's clothes so as to look like a small hogshead.

By and by, the men built a dam to get plenty of water in winter for the rotting of the flax stalks. The linen industry made the people rich. In time, a city sprang up, which they called Rotterdam, or the dam where they rotted the flax.

And, because where had been a forest of oaks, with the pool and rivulet, there was now a silvery stream flowing gently between verdant meadows, they made the arms and seal of the city green and white, two of the former and one of the latter; that is, verdure and silver. To this day, on the arms and flags of the great city, and on the high smoke-stacks of the mighty steamers that cross the ocean, from land to land, one sees the wide, white band between the two broad stripes of green.

THE CAT AND THE CRADLE

In the early ages, when our far-off ancestors lived in the woods, ate acorns, slept in caves, and dressed in the skins of wild animals, they had no horses, cows or cats. Their only pets and helpers were dogs. The men and the dogs were more like each other than they are now.

However, they knew about bees. So the women gathered honey and from it they made mead. Not having any sugar, the children enjoyed tasting honey more than anything else, and it was the only sweet thing they had.

By and by, cows were brought into the country and the Dutch soil being good for grass, the cows had plenty to eat. When these animals multiplied, the people drank milk and learned to make cheese and butter. So the Dutch boys and girls grew fat and healthy.

The oxen were so strong that they could pull logs of wood or draw a plough. So, little by little, the forests were cut down and grassy meadows, full of bright colored flowers, took their place. Houses were built and the people were rich and happy.

Yet there were still many cruel men and bad people in the land. Sometimes, too, floods came and drowned the cattle and covered the fields with sand, or salt water. In such times, food was very scarce. Thus it happened that not all the babies born could live, or every little child be fed. The baby girls especially were often left to die, because war was common and only boys, that grew into strong warriors, were wanted.

It grew to be a custom that families would hold a council and decide whether the baby should be raised or not. But if any one should give the infant even a tiny drop of milk, or food of any kind, it was allowed to live and grow up. If no one gave it milk or honey, it died. No matter how much a mother might love her baby, she was not allowed to put milk to its lips, if the grandmother or elders forbade it. The young bride, coming into her husband's home, always had to obey his mother, for she was now as a daughter and one of the family. All lived together in one house, and the grandmother ruled all the women and girls that were under one roof.

This was the way of the world, when our ancestors were pagans, and not always as kind to little babies as our own mothers and fathers are now.

Many times was the old grandmother angry, when her son had taken a wife and a girl was born. If the old woman expected a grandson, who should grow up and be a fighter, with sword and spear, and it turned out to be a girl, she was mad as fire. Often the pretty bride, brought into the house, had a hard time of it, with her husband's mother, if she did not in time have a baby boy. In those days a "Herman," a "War Man" and "German" were one and the same word.

Now when the good missionaries came into Friesland, one of the first of the families to receive the gospel was one named Altfrid. With his bride, who also became a Christian, Altfrid helped the missionary to build a church. By and by, a sweet little baby was born in the family and the parents were very happy. They loved the little thing sent from God, as fathers and mothers love their children now.

But when some one went and told the pagan grandmother that the new baby was a girl instead of a boy, the old woman flew into a rage and would have gone at once to get hold of the baby and put it to death. Her lameness, however, made her move slowly, and she could not find her crutch; for the midwife, who knew the bad temper of the grandmother, had purposely hid it. The old woman was angry, because she did not want any more females in the big house, where she thought there were already too many mouths to fill. Food was hard to get, and there were not enough war men to defend the tribe. She meant to get the new baby and throw it to the wolves. The old grandmother was a pagan and still worshipped the cruel gods that loved fighting. She hated the new religion, because it taught gentleness and peace.

But the midwife, who was a neighbor, feared that the old woman was malicious and she had hid her crutch. This she did, so that if the baby was a girl, she could save its life. The midwife was a good woman, who had been taught that the Great Creator loves little girls as well as boys.

So when the midwife heard the grandmother storm and rave, while hunting for her crutch, she ran first to the honey jar, dipped her forefinger in it and put some drops of honey on the baby's tongue. Then she passed it out the window to some women friends, who were waiting outside. She knew the law, that if a child tasted food, it must be allowed to live.

The kind women took the baby to their home and fed it carefully. A hole was drilled in the small end of a cow's horn and the warm milk, fresh from the cow, was allowed to fall, drop by drop, into the baby's mouth. In a few days the little one was able to suck its breakfast slowly out of the horn, while one of the girls held it. So the baby grew bigger every day. All the time it was carefully hidden.

The foolish old grandmother was foiled, for she could never find out where the baby girl was, which all the time was growing strong and plump. Her father secretly made her a cradle and he and the babe's mother came often to see their child. Every one called her Honig-je', or Little Honey.

Now about this time, cats were brought into the country and the children made such pets of them that some of the cows seemed to be jealous of the attentions paid to Pussy and the kittens. These were the days when cows and people all lived under one long roof. The children learned to tell the time of day, whether it was morning, noon or night by looking into the cats' eyes. These seemed to open and shut, very much as if they had doors.

The fat pussy, which was brought into the house where Honig-je' was, seemed to be very fond of the little girl, and the two, the cat and the child, played much together. It was often said that the cat loved the baby even more than her own kittens. Every one called the affectionate animal by the nickname of Dub-belt-je', which means Little Double; because this puss was twice as loving as most cat mothers are. When her own furry little babies were very young, she carried them from one place to another in her mouth. But this way, of holding kittens, she never tried on the baby. She seemed to know better. Indeed, Dub-belt-je' often wondered why human babies were born so naked and helpless; for at an age when her kittens could feed themselves and run about and play with their tails and with each other, Honig-je' was not yet able to crawl.

But other dangers were in store for the little girl. One day, when the men were out hunting, and the women went to the woods to gather nuts and acorns, a great flood came. The waters washed away the houses, so that everything floated into the great river, and then down towards the sea.

What had, what would, become of our baby? So thought the parents of Honig-je', when they came back to find the houses swept away and no sign of their little daughter. Dub-belt-je' and her kittens, and all the cows, were gone too.

Now it had happened that when the flood came and the house crashed down, baby was sound asleep. The cat, leaving its kittens, that were now pretty well grown up, leaped up and on to the top of the cradle and the two floated off together. Pretty soon they found themselves left alone, with nothing in sight that was familiar, except one funny thing. That was a wooden shoe, in which was a fuzzy little yellow chicken hardly four days old. It had been playing in the shoe, when the floods came and swept it off from under the very beak of the old hen, that, with all her other chicks, was speedily drowned.

On and on, the raging flood bore baby and puss, until dark night came down. For hours more they drifted until, happily, the cradle was swept into an eddy in front of a village. There it spun round and round, and might soon have been borne into the greater flood, which seemed to roar louder as the waters rose.

Now a cat can see sometimes in the night, better even than in the day, for the darker it becomes, the wider open the eyes of puss. In bright sunshine, at noon, the inside doors of the cat's eyes close to a narrow slit, while at night these doors open wide. That is the reason why, in the days before clocks and watches were made, the children could tell about the time of day by looking at the cat's eyes. Sometimes they named their pussy Klok'-oog, which means Clock Eye, or Bell Eye, for bell clocks are older than clocks with a dial, and because in Holland the bells ring out the hours and quarter hours.

Puss looked up and saw the church tower looming up in the dark. At once she began to meouw and caterwaul with all her might. She hoped that some one in one of the houses near the river bank might catch the sound. But none seemed to hear or heed. At last, when Puss was nearly dead with howling, a light appeared at one of the windows. This showed that some one was up and moving. It was a boy, who was named Dirck, after the saint Theodoric, who had first, long ago, built a church in the village. Then Puss opened her mouth and lungs again and set up a regular cat-scream. This wakened all her other relatives in the village and every Tom and Kitty made answer, until there was a cat concert of meouws and caterwauls.

The boy heard, rushed down-stairs, and, opening the door, listened. The wind blew out his candle, but the brave lad was guided by the sound which Pussy made. Reaching the bank, he threw off his wooden klomps, plunged into the boiling waters, and, seizing the cradle, towed it ashore. Then he woke up his mother and showed her his prize. The way that baby laughed and crowed, and patted the horn of milk, and kicked up its toes in delight over the warm milk, which was brought, was a joy to see. Near the hearth, in the middle of the floor, Dub-belt-je', the puss, was given some straw for a bed and, after purring joyfully, was soon, like the baby, sound asleep.

Thus the cat warned the boy, and the boy saved the baby, that was very welcome in a family where there were no girls, but only a boy. When Honig-je' grew up to be a young woman, she looked as lovely as a princess and in the church was married to Dirck! It was the month of April and all the world was waking to flowers, when the wedding procession came out of the church and the air was sweet with the opening of the buds.

Before the next New Year's day arrived, there lay in the same cradle, and put to sleep over the same rockers, a baby boy. When they brought him to the font, the good grandmother named him Luid-i-ger. He grew up to be the great missionary, whose name in Friesland is, even today, after a thousand years, a household word. He it was who drove out bad fairies, vile enchanters, wicked spirits and terrible diseases. Best of all, he banished "eye-bite," which was the name the people gave to witchcraft. Luid-i-ger, also, made it hard for the naughty elves and sprites that delude men.

After this, it was easy for all the good spirits, that live in kind hearts and noble lives, to multiply and prosper. The wolves were driven away or killed off and became very few, while the cattle and sheep multiplied, until everybody could have a woollen coat, and there was a cow to every person in the land.

But the people still suffered from the floods, that from time to time drowned the cattle and human beings, and the ebb tides, that carried everything out to sea. Then the good missionary taught the men how to build dykes, that kept out the ocean and made the water of the rivers stay between the banks. The floods became fewer and fewer and at last rarely happened. Then Santa Klaas arrived, to keep alive in the hearts of the people the spirit of love and kindness and good cheer forever.

At last, when nearly a hundred years had passed away, Honig-je', once the girl baby, and then the dear old lady, who was kind to everybody and prepared the way for Santa Klaas, died. Then, also, Dub-belt-je' the cat, that had nine lives in one, died with her. They buried the old lady under the church floor and stuffed the pussy that everybody, kittens, boys, girls and people loved. By and by, when the cat's tail and fur fell to pieces, and ears tumbled off, and its glass eyes dropped out, a skilful artist chiselled a statue of Dub-belt-je', which still stands over the tomb in the church. Every year, on Santa Klaas day, December sixth, the children put a new collar around its neck and talk about the cat that saved a baby's life.

PRINCE SPIN HEAD AND MISS SNOW WHITE

Long, long ago, before the Romans came into the land and when the fairies ruled in the forest, there was a maiden who lived under an oak tree. When she was a baby they called her Bundlekin. She had four brothers, who loved their younger sister very dearly and did everything they could to make her happy. Her fat father was a famous hunter. When he roamed the woods, no bear, wolf, aurochs, roebuck, deer, or big animal of any kind, could escape from his arrows, his spear, or his pit-trap. He taught his sons to be skilful in the chase, but also to be kind to the dumb creatures when captured. Especially when the mother beast was killed, the boys were always told to care for the cubs, whelps and kittens. As for the smaller animals, foxes, hares, weasels, rabbits and ermine, these were so numerous, that the father left the business of hunting them to the lads, who had great sport.

The house under the oak tree was always well provided with meat and furs. The four brothers brought the little animals, which they took in the woods, to make presents to their sister. So there was always a plenty of pets, bear and wolf cubs, wildcats' kittens and baby aurochs for the girl to play with. Every day, while the animals were so young as to be fed on milk, she enjoyed frolicking with the four-footed babies. When they grew bigger, she romped and sported with them, as if she and they were equal members of the same family. The older brother watched carefully, so that the little brutes, as they increased in size, should not bite or claw his sister, for he knew the fierce nature that was in wild creatures. Yet the maiden had wonderful power over these beasts of the forest, whether little or big. She was not very much afraid of them and often made them run, by looking at them hard in the eye.

While the girl made a pet of the animals, her parents made a pet of her. The mother prepared the skins of the wolves and bears, until these were very soft, keeping the fur on, to make rugs for the floor, and winter coats for her children. The hides of the aurochs sufficed for rougher use, but from what had once been the clothes of the fawn, the weasel, the rabbit, and the ermine, garments were made that were smooth enough to suit a baby's tender flesh. The forest folk wrapped their infants in swaddling hands made of these dressed pelts. After feeding the darling, a mother hung her baby up, warmly covered, to a tree branch. The cradle, which was a furry bag, was made of the same material and swung in the wind.

Bundlekin usually fell asleep right after she had had her breakfast. When she woke up crowing, the squirrels were playing all around her. She even learned to watch the spiders, spinning their houses of silk, without being afraid. When Bundlekin grew up, she always called this curious creature, that could make silk, Spin Head. She jokingly called it her lover, in remembrance of baby days. It was funny to see how deft the mother was with her needles, fashioned from bone, and her rough thread, which was made of the intestines of the deer. From her own childhood in the woods, Bundlekin's mother had been used to this kind of dressmaking. Now, when her daughter had grown, from babyhood and through her teens, to be a lovely maiden, fair of face and strong of limb, her sweet, unselfish parent was equal to new tasks. To the soft leather coats, made from the skins of fawns, martens, and weasels, she added trimmings of snow white ermine. Caps and mittens, cloaks for the body, and coverings for the feet, were fashioned to fit neatly. Fringes, here and there, were put on them, until her girl looked like a king's daughter. In summer, the skins of birds and their feathers clothed her lightly, and with many and rich colors, while the forest flowers decked her hair.

In winter, in her white forest robes, the maiden, except for her rosy face and sparkling eyes, seemed as if she might have been born of the snow, or was a daughter of the northern ice god at Ulrum. And because she was so lovely, her parents changed her baby name and called her Dri'-fa, which means Snow White.

Yet, though no other girl in Gelderland equalled, and none, not even the princesses, excelled Snow White in beauty of face, form, or raiment, the maiden was not happy, even though many lovers came to her and offered to marry her. Some, as proof of their skill as hunters, brought the finest furs the forest furnished. Others showed their strength or fleetness of foot. Some bargained with the kabouters, or fairies of the mines, to bring them shining ore or precious gems which they offered to Snow White. Others, again, went afar to get strange wonders, amber and ambergris, from the seashores of the far north to please her. One fine fellow, who had been in the south and was proud of his travels, told her of what he had seen in the great cities, and offered her a necklace of pearls.

But all was in vain. Every lover went away sorrowful, for Snow White wearied of them and sent each one home, disappointed.

Last of all, among the lovers came a strange looking one, named Spin Head, resembling a spider, promising a secret worth more than furs, gold, gems, or necklace; but the mother, seeing the ugly creature, drove it off with hard words.

So the months and years passed, until her father feared he would not live to see his daughter a wife.

But one day, when all in the household were absent, the leaves of the oak tree rustled loudly. There was no wind, and Snow White, surprised, strained her ears to find out what this might mean. Soon she could make out these words:

"When the spider, that you called Spin Head, comes to make love to you, listen to him. He is the wisest being in all the forest. He knows the future. He will tell you a secret. I shall pass away, but what he teaches you shall live."

Then the leaves of the oak ceased to rustle and all was quiet and still again.

While wondering what this message might mean, down came the real spider she had named Spin Head. He lowered himself from a tree branch, high above on a silken thread. The creature sat down on the log beside the maiden; but she was not in the least startled and did not scream nor run away. Indeed, she spoke to the spider as an old friend:

"Well, playmate of my babyhood, what have you to tell me?"

"I came to offer you my love. You need not marry me yet, but if you will let me spin a web in your room, I shall live there, and, by and by, reward you. Let me be in your sight always, and you will not be sorry for it."

The maiden had no sooner agreed than a terrible tempest uprooted the oak and levelled the trees of the forest. In a moment more, a new and very beautiful house rose up out of the ground. It was as noble to look at as a palace. Near by was a garden, and one day when she walked in it, out of it sprang a blue flower, almost under her feet.

"Choose the best room for your own self," said Spin Head, "and then show me my corner. After a hundred days, if you treat me kindly, I shall reveal the secret of that blue flower."

Dri'-fa, the maiden, chose the sunniest room, and gave Spin Head the best corner, near the window and close to the ceiling. At once he began to weave a shining web for his own house. She wondered at such fine work, which no human weaver could excel, and why she was not able to spin silk out of her head, nor even with her fingers, like her strange lover. But the oak had promised that Spin Head would reveal a secret, and she was curious to know what it was. Like all girls, she was in a hurry to have the secret. To ease her impatience, Dri'-fa looked on, while Spin Head was thus busy at making his dwelling place, with shining threads which he spun out, never ceasing. She was so intent upon watching him that night came down before she noticed that her room was not furnished. There was not even a bed to sleep on.

Spin Head looked at her closely and then spoke with a deep voice, like a man's:

"Ah, I know, you want a bed, and pretty things for your room."

In another moment, soft furs lined the floor, and soon all that Dri'-fa had possessed in the forest for comfort she had now, and more. Lost in wonder as she was, in a few minutes she was fast asleep.

She dreamed she wore a dress of some strange, new, white fabric, such as her people had never seen before. Instead of being close in texture, like the skin of an animal, it was as open work, full of thousands of little holes, yet strongly held together. It was light and gauzy, like a silvery spider's web on the summer grass before sunrise, when pearly with dewdrops.

The hundred days were passing swiftly by, and Spin Head and Snow White had become fast friends. Each lived in a different world--a world within a world. She was waiting for the secret he would tell her. She bravely resolved not to be impatient, but let Spin Head speak first.

One day, when autumn had come and she was lonely, she sauntered out into the garden. The chill winds were blowing and the leaves falling, till they covered the ground like a yellow carpet. One fell into her hand, as if it bore words of friendly greeting. Yet, though she waited, not one of the millions of them brought a message to her! Never a word had she ever heard from her parents and brothers! The blue flower had long ago fallen away and there was nothing in its place but a hard, rough, black stalk. Then she said to herself:

"Is there anything in this ugly stick? How will Spin Head reveal his secret?" Never had she been so cast down.

Again the tempest howled. All the winds of heaven seemed to have broken loose. Many a sturdy oak lay prostrate. The leaves darkened the air, so that Snow White could see nothing. Then there was a great calm. The maid cleared her sight, and lo! there, beside her, stood a youth, more beautiful than any of her brothers, or her lovers, or any man she had ever seen. He was dressed in fine white clothing, excelling in its texture any skin of fawn, or animal of the forest. Instead of being leather, however soft, it seemed woven of a multitude of threads. In his hand he held the black stalk of what had been the blue flower.

"I am Spin Head," he said. "The hundred days are over. The spell is broken and my deliverance from enchantment has come. I bring to you, as my gift, this ugly stalk, on which the blue flower bloomed."

Between surprise at the change of Spin Head from a spider to a handsome youth, and disappointment at such a present offered her, Snow White was dumb. She could hardly draw her breath. Was that all?

"Break it open," said Spin Head.

Splitting the stalk from end to end, the maiden was surprised to find inside many long silky fibres, almost as fine as the strands in a spider's web. She pulled them out and her eyes danced with joy.

"Plant the seed and let the blue flowers blossom by the million," said the youth. "Then gather the stalks and, from the fibres, weave them together and make this. The black rod is a sceptre of wealth."

Then, separating the delicate strands one by one, Spin Head wove them together. The result was a rich robe, of a snow white fabric, never seen in the forest. It was linen.

Snow White clapped her hands with joy.

"'Tis for your wedding dress, if you will marry me," said Spin Head.

Snow White's cheeks blushed red, but she looked at him and her eyes said "yes."

"Wait," said Spin Head. "I'll make you a bridal veil."

Once more his fingers wrought wonders. He produced yards of a gauzy, open work stuff. He made it float in the air first. Then he threw it over her head. It trailed down her back and covered her rosy face. It was lace.

Happily married, they left the forest and travelled into the land where the blue flax flowers made a new sky on the earth. Soon on the map men read the names of cities unknown before. At a time when Europe had no such masses of happy people, joyous in their toil, Courtrai, Tournay, Ypres, Ghent, and Bruges told what the blue flower of the flax had done for the country. More than gold, gems, or the wealth of forest or mine, was the gift of Spin Head to Snow White, for the making of Belgic Land.

THE BOAR WITH THE GOLDEN BRISTLES

Long, long ago, there were brave fighters and skilful hunters in Holland, but neither men nor women ever dreamed that food was to be got out of the ground, but only from the trees and bushes, such as berries, acorns and honey. They thought the crust of the earth was too hard to be broken up for seed, even if they knew what grain and bread were. They supposed that what nature provided in the forest was the only food for men. Besides this, they made their women do all the work and cook the acorns and brew the honey into mead, while they went out to fish and hunt and fight.

So the fairies took pity on the cold, northern people, who lived where it rained and snowed a great deal. They held a council and agreed that it was time to send down to the earth an animal, with tusks, to tear up the ground. Then the people would see the riches of the earth and learn what soil was. They would be blessed with farms and gardens, barns and stalls, hay and grain, horses and cattle, wheat and barley, pigs and clover.

Now there were powerful fairies, of a certain kind, who lived in a Happy Land far, far away, who had charge of everything in the air and water. One of them was named Fro, who became lord of the summer sunshine and warm showers, that make all things grow. It was in this bright region that the white elves lived.

It was a pretty custom in fairy-land that when a fairy baby cut its first tooth, the mother's friends should make the little one some pretty present.

When Nerthus, the mother of the infant Fro, looked into its mouth and saw the little white thing that had come up through the baby's gums, she went in great glee and told the glad news to all the other fairies. It was a great event and she tried to guess what present her wonderful boy-baby should receive.

There was one giant-like fairy as strong as a polar bear, who agreed to get, for little Fro, a creature that could put his nose under the sod and root up the ground. In this way he would show men what the earth, just under its surface, contained, without their going into mines and caverns.

One day this giant fairy heard two stout dwarfs talking loudly in the region under the earth. They were boasting as to which could beat the other at the fire and bellows, for both were blacksmiths. One was the king of the dwarfs, who made a bet that he could excel the other. So he set them to work as rivals, while a third dwarf worked the bellows. The dwarf-king threw some gold in the flames to melt; but, fearing he might not win the bet, he went away to get other fairies to help him. He told the bellows dwarf to keep on pumping air on the fire, no matter what might happen to him.

So when one giant fairy, in the form of a gadfly, flew at him, and bit him in the hand, the bellows-blower did not stop for the pain, but kept on until the fire roared loudly, as to make the cavern echo. Then all the gold melted and could be transformed. As soon as the dwarf-king came back, the bellows-blower took up the tongs and drew out of the fire a boar having golden bristles.

This fire-born golden boar had the power of travelling through the air as swiftly as a streak of lightning. It was named Gullin, or Golden, and was given to the fairy Fro, and he, when grown, used the wonderful creature as his steed. All the other good fairies and the elves rejoiced, because men on the earth would now be helped to do great things.

Even more wonderful to tell, this fire-born creature became the father of all the animals that have tusks and that roam in the woods. A tusk is a big tooth, of which the hardest and sharpest part grows, long and sharp, outside of the mouth and it stays there, even when the mouth is shut.

When Gullin was not occupied, or being ridden by Fro on his errands over the world, he taught his sons, that is, the wild boars of the forest, how to root up the ground and make it soft for things to grow in. Then his master Fro sent the sunbeams and the warm showers to make the turned-up earth fruitful.

To do this, the wild boars were given two long tusks, as pointed as needles and sharp as knives. With one sweep of his head a boar could rip open a dog or a wolf, a bull or a bear, or furrow the earth like a ploughshare.

Now there were several cousins in the Tusk family. The elephant on land, and the walrus and narwhal in the seas; but none of these could plough ground, but because the boar's tusks grew out so long and were so sharp, and hooked at the end, it could tear open the earth's hard crust and root up the ground. This made a soil fit for tender plants to grow in, and even the wild flowers sprang up in them.

All this, when they first noticed it, was very wonderful to human beings. The children called one to the other to come and see the unusual sight. The little troughs, made first by the ripping of the boar's tusks, were widened by rooting with their snouts. These were welcomed by the birds, for they hopped into the lines thus made, to feed on the worms. So the birds, supposing that these little gutters in the ground were made especially for them, made great friends with the boars. They would even perch near by, or fly to their backs, and ride on them.

As for the men fathers, when they looked at the clods and the loose earth thus turned over, they found them to be very soft. So the women and girls were able to break them up with their sticks. Then the seeds, dropped by the birds that came flying back every spring time, from far-away lands, sprouted. It was noticed that new kinds of plants grew up, which had stalks. In the heads or ears of these were a hundredfold more seeds. When the children tasted them, they found, to their delight, that the little grains were good to eat. They swallowed them whole, they roasted them at the fire, or they pounded them with stones. Then they baked the meal thus made or made it into mush, eating it with honey.

For the first time people in the Dutch world had bread. When they added the honey, brought by the bees, they had sweet cakes with mead. Then, saving the seeds over, from one summer to another, they in the spring time planted them in the little trenches made by the animal's tusks. Then the Dutch words for "boar" and "row" were put together, meaning boar row, and there issued, in time, our word "furrow."

The women were the first to become skilful in baking. In the beginning they used hot stones on which to lay the lump of meal, or flour and water, or the batter. Then having learned about yeast, which "raised" the flour, that is, lifted it up, with gas and bubbles, they made real bread and cakes and baked them in the ovens which the men had made. When they put a slice of meat between upper and lower layers of bread, they called it "broodje," that is, little bread; or, sandwich. In time, instead of one kind of bread, or cake, they had a dozen or twenty different sorts, besides griddle cakes and waffles.

Now when the wise men of the mark, or neighborhood, saw that the women did such wonderful things, they put their heads together and said one to the other:

"We are quite ready to confess that fairies, and elves, and even the kabouters are smarter than we are. Our women, also, are certainly wonderful; but it will never do to let the boars think that they know more than we do. They did indeed teach us how to make furrows, and the birds brought us grain; but we are the greater, for we can hunt and kill the boars with our spears.

"Although they can tear up the sod and root in the ground with tusk and snout, they cannot make cakes, as our women can. So let us see if we cannot beat both the boars and birds, and even excel our women. We shall be more like the fairies, if we invent something that will outshine them all."

So they thought and planned, and, little by little, they made the plough. First, with a sharp stick in their hands, the men scratched the surface of the ground into lines that were not very deep. Then they nailed plates of iron on those sticks. Next, they fixed this iron-shod wood in a frame to be pulled forward, and, by and by, they added handles. Men and women, harnessed together, pulled the plough. Indeed it was ages before they had oxen to do this heavy work for them. At last the perfect plough was seen. It had a knife in front to cut the clods, a coulter, a beam, a mould board and handles, and, after a while, a wheel to keep it straight. Then they set horses to draw it.

Fro the fairy was the owner, not only of the boar with the golden bristles, but also of the lightning-like horse, Sleipnir, that could ride through fire and water with the speed of light. Fro also owned the magic ship, which could navigate both land and sea. It was so very elastic that it could be stretched out to carry a host of warriors over the seas to war, or fold up like a lady's handkerchief. With this flying vessel, Fro was able to move about like a cloud and also to change like them. He could also appear, or disappear, as he pleased, in one place or another.

By and by, the wild boars were all hunted to death and disappeared. Yet in one way, and a glorious one also, their name and fame were kept in men's memories. Brave knights had the boar's head painted on their shields and coats of arms. When the faith of the Prince of Peace made wars less frequent, the temples in honor of Fro were deserted, but the yule log and the revels, held to celebrate the passing of the Mother Night, in December, that is, the longest one of the year, were changed for the Christmas festival.

Then again, the memory of man's teacher of the plough was still kept green; for the boar was remembered as the giver, not only of nourishing meat, but of ideas for men's brains. Baked in the oven, and made delightful to the appetite, served on the dish, with its own savory odors; withal, decorated with sprigs of rosemary, the boar's head was brought in for the great dinner, with the singing of Christmas carols.

THE ICE KING AND HIS WONDERFUL GRANDCHILD

In the far-off ages, all the lands of northern Europe were one, for the deep seas had not yet separated them. Then our forefathers thought that fairies were gods. They built temples in their honor, and prayed to them. Then, in the place where is now the little town of Ulrum in Friesland was the home of the spirit in the ice, Uller. That is what Ulrum means, the home of the good fairy Uller.

Uller was the patron of boys and girls. They liked him, because he invented skates and sleds and sleighs. He had charge of things in winter and enjoyed the cold. He delighted also in hunting. Dressed in thick furs, he loved to roam over the hills and through the forests, seeking out the wolf, the bear, the deer, and the aurochs. His bow and arrows were terrible, for they were very big and he was a sure shot. Being the patron of archery, hunters always sought his favor. The yew tree was sacred to Uller, because the best bows were made from its wood. No one could cut down a yew tree without angering Uller.

Nobody knew who Uller's father was, and if he knew himself, he did not care to tell any one. He would not bestow many blessings upon mankind; yet thousands of people used to come to Ulrum every year to invoke his aid and ask him to send a heavy fall of snow to cover the ground. That meant good crops of food for the next year. The white snow, lying thick upon the ground, kept back the frost giants from biting the earth too hard. Because of deep winter snows, the ground was soft during the next summer. So the seed sprouted more easily and there was plenty to eat.

When Uller travelled over the winter snow, to go out on hunting trips, he strapped snow-shoes on his feet. Because these were shaped like a warrior's shield, Uller was often called the shield-god. His protection was especially invoked by men who fought duels with sword or spear, which were very common in early days; or by soldiers or hunters, who wished to be very brave, or had engaged in perilous ventures.

Now when Uller wanted a wife to marry him, he made love to Skadi, because she was a huntress and liked the things which he liked. So they never had a quarrel. She was very strong, fond of sports, and of chasing the wild animals. She wore a short skirt, which allowed freedom of motion to her limbs. Then she ranged over the hills and valleys with wonderful swiftness. So rapid were her movements that many people likened her to the cold mountain stream, that leaps down from the high peaks and over the rocks, foaming and dashing to the lowlands. They gave the same name to both this fairy woman and the water, because they were so much alike.

Indeed Skadi was very lovely to look at. It was no wonder that many of the gods, fairies and men fell in love with her. It is even said that she had had several husbands before marrying Uller. When you look at her pictures, you will see that she was as pretty as bright winter itself, when Jack Frost clothes the trees with white and makes the cheeks of the girls so rosy. She wore armor of shining steel, a silver helmet, short white skirts and white fur leggings. Her snow-shoes were of the hue of winter. Besides a glittering spear, she had a bow and sharp arrows. These were held in a silver quiver slung over her shoulders. Altogether, she looked like winter alive. She loved to live in the mountains, and hear the thunders of cataracts, the crash of avalanches, the moaning of the winds in the pine forests. Even the howling of wolves was music in her ears. She was afraid of nothing.

Now from such a father and mother one would expect wonderful children, yet very much like their parents. It turned out that the offspring of Uller and Skadi were all daughters. To them--one after another--were given the names meaning Glacier, Cold, Snow, Drift, Snow Whirl, and Snow Dust, the oldest being the biggest and hardiest. The others were in degree softer and more easily influenced by the sun and the wind. They all looked alike, so that some people called them the Six White Sisters.

Yet they were all so great and powerful that many considered them giantesses. It was not possible for men to tame them, for they did very much as they pleased. No one could stop their doings or drive them away, except Woden, who was the god of the sun. Yet in winter, even he left off ruling the world and went away. During that time, that is, during seven months, Uller took Woden's throne and governed the affairs of the world. When summer came, Uller went with his wife up to the North Pole; or they lived in a house, on the top of the Alps. There they could hunt and roam on their snow-shoes. To these cold places, which the whole family enjoyed, their daughters went also and all were very happy so far above the earth.

Things went on pleasantly in Uller's family so long as his daughters were young, for then the girls found enough to delight in at their daily play. But when grown up and their heads began to be filled with notions about the young giants, who paid visits to them, then the family troubles began.

There was one young giant fairy named Vuur, who came often to see all six of Uller's daughters, from the youngest to the oldest. Yet no one could tell which of them he was in love with, or could name the girl he liked best; no, not even the daughters themselves. His character and his qualities were not well known, for he put on many disguises and appeared in many places. It was believed, however, that he had already done a good deal of mischief and was likely to do more, for he loved destruction. Yet he often helped the kabouter dwarfs to do great things; so that showed he was of some use. In fact he was the fire fairy. He kept on, courting all the six sisters, long after May day came, and he lengthened his visits until the heat turned the entire half dozen of them into water. So they became one.

At this, Uller was so angry at Vuur's having delayed so long before popping the question, and at his daughters' losing their shapes, that he made Vuur marry them all and at once, they taking the name of Regen.

Now when the child of Vuur and Regen was born, it turned out to be, in body and in character, just what people expected from such a father and mother. It was named in Dutch, Stoom. It grew fast and soon showed that it was as powerful as its parents had been; yet it was much worse, when shut up, than when allowed to go free in the air. Stoom loved to do all sorts of tricks. In the kitchen, it would make the iron kettle lid flop up and down with a lively noise. If it were confined in a vessel, whether of iron or earthenware, when set over the fire, it would blow the pot or kettle all to pieces, in order to get out. Thinking itself a great singer, it would make rather a pleasant sound, when its mother let it come out of a spout. Yet it never obeyed either of its parents. When they tried to shut up Stoom inside of anything, it always escaped with a terrible sound. In fact, nothing could long hold it in, without an explosion.

Sometimes Stoom would go down into the bowels of the earth and turn on a stream of water so as to meet the deep fires which are ever burning far down below us. Then there would come an awful earthquake, because Stoom wanted to get out, and the earth crust would not let him, but tried to hold him down. Sometimes Stoom slipped down into a volcano's mouth. Then the mountain, in order to save itself from being choked, had to spit Stoom out, and this always made a terrible mess on the ground, and men called it lava. Or, Stoom might stay down in the crater as a guest, and quietly come out, occasionally, in jets and puffs.

Even when Jack Frost was around and froze the pipes in the house, or turned the water of the pots, pans, kettles and bottles into solid ice, Stoom behaved very badly. If the frozen kettles, or any other closed vessel were put over the stove, or near the fire, and the ice melted at the bottom too fast,

Stoom would blow the whole thing up. In this way, he often put men's lives in danger and made them lose their property.

No one seemed to know how to handle this mischievous fairy. Not one man on earth could do anything with him. So they let him have his own way. Yet all the time, though he was enjoying his own tricks and lively fun, he was, with his own voice, calling on human beings to use him properly, and harness him to wheels; for he was willing to be useful to them, and was all ready to pull or drive, lift or lower, grind or pump, as the need might be.

As long as men did not treat him properly and give him the right to get out into the air, after he had done his work, Stoom would explode, blow up and destroy everything. He could be made to sing, hiss, squeal, whistle, and make all kinds of sounds, but, unless the bands that held him in were strong enough, or if Vuur got too hot, or his mother would not give him drink enough, when the iron pipes were red with heat, he would lose his temper and explode. He had no respect for bad or neglected boilers, or for lazy or careless firemen and engineers.

Yet properly harnessed and treated well, and fed with the food such as his mother can give, and roused by his father's persuasion, Stoom is greater than any giant or fairy that ever was. He can drive a ship, a locomotive, a submarine, or an aeroplane, as fast as Fro's boar, horse or ship. Everybody to-day is glad that Stoom is such a good servant and friend all over the world.

THE ELVES AND THEIR ANTICS

The elves are the little white creatures that live between heaven and earth. They are not in the clouds, nor down in the caves and mines, like the kabouters. They are bright and fair, dwelling in the air, and in the world of light. The direct heat of the sun is usually too much for them, so they are not often seen during the day, except towards sunset. They love the silvery moonlight. There used to be many folks, who thought they had seen the beautiful creatures, full of fun and joy, dancing hand in hand, in a circle.

In these old days, long since gone by, there were more people than there are now, who were sure they had many times enjoyed the sight of the elves. Some places in Holland show, by their names, where this kind of fairies used to live. These little creatures, that looked as thin as gauze, were very lively and mischievous, though they often helped honest and hard working people in their tasks, as we shall see. But first and most of all, they were fond of fun. They loved to vex cross people and to please those who were bonnie and blithe. They hated misers, but they loved the kind and generous. These little folks usually took their pleasure in the grassy meadows, among the flowers and butterflies. On bright nights they played among the moonbeams.

There were certain times when the elves were busy, in such a way as to make men and girls think about them. Then their tricks were generally in the stable, or in the field among the cows. Sometimes, in the kitchen or dairy, among the dishes or milk-pans, they made an awful mess for the maids to clean up. They tumbled over the churns, upset the milk jugs, and played hoops with the round cheeses. In a bedroom they made things look as if the pigs had run over them.

When a farmer found his horse's mane twisted into knots, or two cows with their tails tied together, he said at once, "That's the work of elves." If the mares did not feel well, or looked untidy, their owners were sure the elves had taken the animals out and had been riding them all night. If a cow was sick, or fell down on the grass, it was believed that the elves had shot an arrow into its body. The inquest, held on many a dead calf or its mother, was, that it died from an "elf-shot." They were so sure of this, that even when a stone arrow head--such as our far-off ancestors used in hunting, when they were cave men--was picked up off the ground, it was called an "elf bolt," or "elf-arrow."

Near a certain village named Elf-berg or Elf Hill, because there were so many of the little people in that neighborhood, there was one very old elf, named Styf, which means Stiff, because though so old he stood up straight as a lance. Even more than the young elves, he was famous for his pranks. Sometimes he was nicknamed Haan-e'-kam or Cock's Comb. He got this name, because he loved to mock the roosters, when they crowed, early in the morning. With his red cap on, he did look like a rooster. Sometimes he fooled the hens, that heard him crowing. Old Styf loved nothing better than to go to a house where was a party indoors. All the wooden shoes of the twenty or thirty people within, men and women, girls and boys, would be left outside the door. All good Dutch folks step out of their heavy timber shoes, or klomps, before they enter a house. It is always a curious sight, at a country church, or gathering of people at a party, to see the klomps, big and little, belonging to baby boys and girls, and to the big men, who wear a number thirteen shoe of wood. One wonders how each one of the owners knows his own, but he does. Each pair is put in its own place, but Old Styf would come and mix them all up together, and then leave them in a pile. So when the people came out to go home, they had a terrible time in finding and sorting out their shoes. Often they scolded each other; or, some innocent boy was blamed for the mischief. Some did not find out, till the next day, that they had on one foot their own, and on another foot, their neighbor's shoe. It usually took a week to get the klomps sorted out, exchanged, and the proper feet into the right shoes. In this way, which was a special trick with him, this naughty elf, Styf, spoiled the temper of many people.

Beside the meadow elves, there were other kinds in Elfin Land; some living in the woods, some in the sand-dunes, but those called Staalkaars, or elves of the stall, were Old Styf's particular friends. These lived in stables and among the cows. The Moss Maidens, that could do anything with leaves, even turning them into money, helped Styf, for they too liked mischief. They teased men-folks, and enjoyed nothing better than misleading the stupid fellows that fuddled their brains with too much liquor.

Styf's especially famous trick was played on misers. It was this. When he heard of any old fellow, who wanted to save the cost of candles, he would get a kabouter to lead him off in the swamps, where the sooty elves come out, on dark nights, to dance. Hoping to catch these lights and use them for candles, the mean fellow would find himself in a swamp, full of water and chilled to the marrow. Then the kabouters would laugh loudly.

Old Styf had the most fun with another stingy fellow, who always scolded children when he found them spending a penny. If he saw a girl buying flowers, or a boy giving a copper coin for a waffle, he talked roughly to them for wasting money. Meeting this miser one day, as he was walking along the brick road, leading from the village, Styf offered to pay the old man a thousand guilders, in exchange for four striped tulips, that grew in his garden. The miser, thinking it real silver, eagerly took the money and put it away in his iron strong box. The next night, when he went, as he did three times a week, to count, and feel, and rub, and gloat, over his cash, there was nothing but leaves in a round form. These, at his touch, crumbled to pieces. The Moss Maidens laughed uproariously, when the mean old fellow was mad about it.

But let no one suppose that the elves, because they were smarter than stupid human beings, were always in mischief. No, no! They did, indeed, have far more intelligence than dull grown folks, lazy boys, or careless girls; but many good things they did. They sewed shoes for poor cobblers, when they were sick, and made clothes for children, when the mother was tired. When they were around, the butter came quick in the churn.

When the blue flower of the flax bloomed in Holland, the earth, in spring time, seemed like the sky. Old Styf then saw his opportunity to do a good thing. Men thought it a great affair to have even coarse linen tow for clothes. No longer need they hunt the wolf and deer in the forest, for their garments. By degrees, they learned to make finer stuff, both linen for clothes and sails for ships, and this fabric they spread out on the grass until the cloth was well bleached. When taken up, it was white as the summer clouds that sailed in the blue sky. All the world admired the product, and soon the word "Holland" was less the name of a country, than of a dainty fabric, so snow white, that it was fit to robe a queen. The world wanted more and more of it, and the Dutch linen weaver grew rich. Yet still there was more to come.

Now, on one moonlight night in summer, the lady elves, beautiful creatures, dressed in gauze and film, with wings to fly and with feet that made no sound, came down into the meadows for their fairy dances. But when, instead of green grass, they saw a white landscape, they wondered, Was it winter?

Surely not, for the air was warm. No one shivered, or was cold. Yet there were whole acres as white as snow, while all the old fairy rings, grass and flowers were hidden.

They found that the meadows had become bleaching grounds, so that the cows had to go elsewhere to get their dinner, and that this white area was all linen. However, they quickly got over their surprise, for elves are very quick to notice things. But now that men had stolen a march on them, they asked whether, after all, these human beings had more intelligence than elves. Not one of these fairies but believed that men and women were the inferiors of elves.

So, then and there, began a battle of wits.

"They have spoiled our dancing floor with their new invention; so we shall have to find another," said the elfin queen, who led the party.

"They are very proud of their linen, these men are; but, without the spider to teach them, what could they have done? Even a wild boar can instruct these human beings. Let us show them, that we, also, can do even more. I'll get Old Styf to put on his thinking cap. He'll add something new that will make them prouder yet."

"But we shall get the glory of it," the elves shouted in chorus. Then they left off talking and began their dances, floating in the air, until they looked, from a distance, like a wreath of stars.

The next day, a procession of lovely elf maidens and mothers waited on Styf and asked him to devise something that would excel the invention of linen; which, after all, men had learned from the spider.

"Yes, and they would not have any grain fields, if they had not learned from the wild boar," added the elf queen.

Old Styf answered "yes" at once to their request, and put on his red thinking cap. Then some of the girl elves giggled, for they saw that he did, really, look like a cock's comb. "No wonder they called him Haan-e'-kam," said one elf girl to the other.

Now Old Styf enjoyed fooling, just for the fun of it, and he taught all the younger elves that those who did the most work with their hands and head, would have the most fun when they were old.

First of all, he went at once to see Fro, the spirit of the golden sunshine and the warm summer showers, who owned two of the most wonderful things in the world. One was his sword, which, as soon as it was drawn out of its sheath, against wicked enemies, fought of its own accord and won every battle. Fro's chief enemies were the frost giants, who wilted the flowers and blasted the plants useful to man. Fro was absent, when Styf came, but his wife promised he would come next day, which he did. He was happy to meet all the elves and fairies, and they, in turn, joyfully did whatever he told them. Fro knew all the secrets of the grain fields, for he could see what was in every kernel of both the stalks and the ripe ears. He arrived, in a golden chariot, drawn by his wild boar which served him instead of a horse. Both chariot and boar drove over the tops of the ears of wheat, and faster than the wind.

The Boar was named Gullin, or Golden Bristles because of its sunshiny color and splendor. In this chariot, Fro had specimens of all the grains, fruits, and vegetables known to man, from which Styf could choose, for these he was accustomed to scatter over the earth.

When Styf told him just what he wanted to do, Fro picked out a sheaf of wheat and whispered a secret in his ear. Then he drove away, in a burst of golden glory, which dazzled even the elves, that loved the bright sunshine. These elves were always glad to see the golden chariot coming or passing by.

Styf also summoned to his aid the kabouters, and, from these ugly little fellows, got some useful hints; for they, dwelling in the dark caverns, know many secrets which men used to name alchemy, and which they now call chemistry.

Then Styf fenced himself off from all intruders, on the top of a bright, sunny hilltop, with his thinking cap on and made experiments for seven days. No elves, except his servants, were allowed to see him. At the end of a week, still keeping his secret and having instructed a dozen or so of the elf girls in his new art, he invited all the elves in the Low Countries to come to a great exhibition, which he intended to give.

What a funny show it was! On one long bench, were half a dozen washtubs; and on a table, near by, were a dozen more washtubs; and on a longer table not far away were six ironing boards, with smoothing irons. A stove, made hot with a peat fire, was to heat the irons. Behind the tubs and tables, stood the twelve elf maidens, all arrayed in shining white garments and caps, as spotless as snow. One might almost think they were white elves of the meadow and not kabouters of the mines. The wonder was that their linen clothes were not only as dainty as stars, but that they glistened, as if they had laid on the ground during a hoar frost.

Yet it was still warm summer. Nothing had frozen, or melted, and the rosy-faced elf-maidens were as dry as an ivory fan. Yet they resembled the lilies of the garden when pearly with dew-drops.

When all were gathered together, Old Styf called for some of the company, who had come from afar, to take off their dusty and travel-stained linen garments and give them to him. These were passed over to the trained girls waiting to receive them. In a jiffy, they were washed, wrung out, rinsed and dried. It was noticed that those elf-maidens, who were standing at the last tub, were intently expecting to do something great, while those five elf maids at the table took off the hot irons from the stove. They touched the bottom of the flat-irons with a drop of water to see if it rolled off hissing.

They kept their eyes fixed on Styf, who now came forward before all and said, in a loud voice:

"Elves and fairies, moss maidens and stall sprites, one and all, behold our invention, which our great friend Fro and our no less helpful friends, the kabouters, have helped me to produce. Now watch me prove its virtues."

Forthwith he produced before all a glistening substance, partly in powder, and partly in square lumps, as white as chalk. He easily broke up a handful under his fingers, and flung it into the fifth tub, which had hot water in it. After dipping the washed garments in the white gummy mass, he took them up, wrung them out, dried them with his breath, and then handed them to the elf ironers. In a few moments, these held up, before the company, what a few minutes before had been only dusty and stained clothes. Now, they were white and resplendent. No fuller's earth could have bleached them thus, nor added so glistening a surface.

It was starch, a new thing for clothes. The fairies, one and all, clapped their hands in delight.

"What shall we name it?" modestly asked Styf of the oldest gnome present.

"Hereafter, we shall call you Styf Sterk, Stiff Starch." They all laughed.

Very quickly did the Dutch folks, men and women, hear and make use of the elves' invention. Their linen closets now looked like piles of snow. All over the Low Countries, women made caps, in new fashions, of lace or plain linen, with horns and wings, flaps and crimps, with quilling and with whirligigs. Soon, in every town, one could read the sign "Hier mangled men" (Here we do ironing).

In time, kings, queens and nobles made huge ruffs, often so big that their necks were invisible, and their heads nearly lost from sight, in rings of quilled linen, or of lace, that stuck out a foot or so. Worldly people dyed their starch yellow; zealous folk made it blue; but moderate people kept it snowy white.

Starch added money and riches to the nation. Kings' treasuries became fat with money gained by taxes laid on ruffs, and on the cargoes of starch, which was now imported by the shipload, or made on the spot, in many countries. So, out of the ancient grain came a new spirit that worked for sweetness and beauty, cleanliness, and health. From a useful substance, as old as Egypt, was born a fine art, that added to the sum of the world's wealth and pleasure.

THE KABOUTERS AND THE BELLS

When the young queen Wilhelmina visited Brabant and Limburg, they amused her with pageants and plays, in which the little fellows called kabouters, in Dutch, and kobolds in German, played and showed off their tricks. Other small folk, named gnomes, took part in the tableaux. The kabouters are the dark elves, who live in forests and mines. The white elves live in the open fields and the sunshine.

The gnomes do the thinking, but the kabouters carry out the work of mining and gathering the precious stones and minerals. They are short, thick fellows, very strong and are strenuous in digging out coal and iron, copper and gold. When they were first made, they were so ugly, that they had to live where they could not be seen, that is, in the dark places. The grown imps look like old men with beards, but no one ever heard of a kabouter that was taller than a yardstick. As for the babies, they are hardly bigger than a man's thumb. The big boys and girls, in the kabouter kingdom, are not much over a foot high.

What is peculiar about them all is, that they help the good and wise people to do things better; but they love to plague and punish the dull folks, that are stupid, or foolish or naughty. In impish glee, they lure the blockheads, or in Dutch, the "cheese-heads," to do worse.

A long time ago, there were no church spires or bells in the land of the Dutch folks, as there are now by the thousands. The good teachers from the South came into the country and taught the people to have better manners, finer clothes and more wholesome food. They also persuaded them to forget their cruel gods and habits of revenge. They told of the Father in Heaven, who loves us all, as his children, and forgives us when we repent of our evil doings.

Now when the chief gnomes and kabouters heard of the newcomers in the land, they held a meeting and said one to the other:

"We shall help all the teachers that are good and kind, but we shall plague and punish the rough fellows among them."

So word was sent to all little people in the mines and hills, instructing them how they were to act and what they were to do.

Some of the new teachers, who were foreigners, and did not know the customs of the country, were very rude and rough. Every day they hurt the feelings of the people. With their axes they cut down the sacred trees. They laughed scornfully at the holy wells and springs of water. They reviled the people, when they prayed to great Woden, with his black ravens that told him everything, or to the gentle Freya, with her white doves, who helped good girls to get kind husbands. They scolded the children at play, and this made their fathers and mothers feel miserable. This is the reason why so many people were angry and sullen, and would not listen to the foreign teachers.

Worse than this, many troubles came to these outsiders. Their bread was sour, when they took it out of the oven. So was the milk, in their pans. Sometimes they found their beds turned upside down. Gravel stones rattled down into their fireplaces. Their hats and shoes were missing. In fact, they had a terrible time generally and wanted to go back home. When the kabouter has a grudge against any one, he knows how to plague him.

But the teachers that were wise and gentle had no trouble. They persuaded the people with kind words, and, just as a baby learns to eat other food at the table, so the people were weaned away from cruel customs and foolish beliefs. Many of the land's folk came to listen to the teachers and helped them gladly to build churches.

More wonderful than this, were the good things that came to these kind teachers, they knew not how. Their bread and milk were always sweet and in plenty. They found their beds made up and their clothes kept clean, gardens planted with blooming flowers, and much hard work done for them. When they would build a church in a village, they wondered how it was that the wood and the nails, the iron necessary to brace the beams, and the copper and brass for the sacred vessels, came so easily and in plenty. When, on some nights, they wondered where they would get food to eat, they found, on waking up in the morning, that there was always something good ready for them. Thus many houses of worship were built, and the more numerous were the churches, the more did farms, cows, grain fields, and happy people multiply.

Now when the gnomes and kabouters, who like to do work for pleasant people, heard that the good teachers wanted church bells, to call the people to worship, they resolved to help the strangers. They would make not only a bell, or a chime, but, actually a carillon, or concert of bells to hang up in the air.

The dark dwarfs did not like to dig metal for swords or spears, or what would hurt people; but the church bells would guide travellers in the forest, and quiet the storms, that destroyed houses and upset boats and killed or drowned people, besides inviting the people to come and pray and sing. They knew that the good teachers were poor and could not buy bells in France or Italy. Even if they had money, they could not get them through the thick forests, or over the stormy seas, for they were too heavy.

When all the kabouters were told of this, they came together to work, night and day, in the mines. With pick and shovel, crowbar and chisel, and hammer and mallet, they broke up the rocks containing copper and tin. Then they built great roaring fires, to smelt the ore into ingots. They would show the teachers that the Dutch kabouters could make bells, as well as the men in the lands of the South. These dwarfish people are jealous of men and very proud of what they can do.

It was the funniest sight to see these short legged fellows, with tiny coats coming just below their thighs, and little red caps, looking like a stocking and ending in a tassel, on their heads, and in shoes that had no laces, but very long points. They flew around as lively as monkeys, and when the fire was hot they threw off everything and worked much harder and longer than men do.

Were they like other fairies? Well, hardly. One must put away all his usual thoughts, when he thinks of kabouters. No filmy wings on their backs! No pretty clothes or gauzy garments, or stars, or crowns, or wands! Instead of these were hammers, pickaxes, and chisels. But how diligent, useful and lively these little folks, in plain, coarse coats and with bare legs, were! In place of things light, clean and easy, the kabouters had furnaces, crucibles and fires of coal and wood.

Sometimes they were grimy, with smoke and coal dust, and the sweat ran down their faces and bodies. Yet there was always plenty of water in the mines, and when hard work was over they washed and looked plain but tidy. Besides their stores of gold, and silver, and precious stones, which they kept ready, to give to good people, they had tools with which to tease or tantalize cruel, mean or lazy folks.

Now when the kabouter daddies began the roaring fires for the making of the bells, the little mothers and the small fry in the kabouter world could not afford to be idle. One and all, they came down from off the earth, and into the mines they went in a crowd. They left off teasing milkmaids, tangling skeins of flax, tearing fishermen's nets, tying knots in cows' tails, tumbling pots, pans and dishes, in the kitchen, or hiding hats, and throwing stones down the chimneys onto the fireplaces. They even ceased their fun of mocking children, who were calling the cows home, by hiding behind the rocks and shouting to them. Instead of these tricks, they saved their breath to blow the fires into a blast. Everybody wondered where the "kabs" were, for on the farms and in town nothing happened and all was as quiet as when a baby is asleep.

For days and weeks underground, the dwarfs toiled, until their skins, already dark, became as sooty as the rafters in the houses of our ancestors. Finally, when all the labor was over, the chief gnomes were invited down into the mines to inspect the work.

What a sight! There were at least a hundred bells, of all sizes, like as in a family; where there are daddy, mother, grown ups, young sons and daughters, little folk and babies, whether single, twins or triplets. Big bells, that could scarcely be put inside a hogshead, bells that would go into a barrel, bells that filled a bushel, and others a peck, stood in rows. From the middle, and tapering down the row, were scores more, some of them no larger than cow-bells. Others, at the end, were so small, that one had to think of pint and gill measures.

Besides all these, there were stacks of iron rods and bars, bolts, nuts, screws, and wires and yokes on which to hang the bells.

One party of the strongest of the kabouters had been busy in the forest, close to a village, where some men, ordered to do so by a foreign teacher, had begun to cut down some of the finest and most sacred of the grand old trees. They had left their tools in the woods; but the "kabs," at night, seized their axes and before morning, without making any noise, they had levelled all but the holy trees. Those they spared. Then, the timber, all cut and squared, ready to hold the bells, was brought to the mouth of the mine.

Now in Dutch, the name for bell is "klok." So a wise and gray-bearded gnome was chosen by the high sounding title of klokken-spieler, or bell player, to test the bells for a carillon. They were all hung, for practice, on the big trestles, in a long row. Each one of these frames was called a "hang," for they were just like those on which fishermen's nets were laid to dry and be mended.

So when all were ready, washed, and in their clean clothes, every one of the kabouter families, daddies, mothers, and young ones, were ranged in lines and made to sing. The heavy male tenors and baritones, the female sopranos and contraltos, the trebles of the little folks, and the squeaks of the very small children, down to the babies' cooing, were all heard by the gnomes, who were judges. The high and mighty klokken-spieler, or master of the carillon, chose those voices with best tone and quality, from which to set in order and regulate the bells.

It was pitiful to see how mad and jealous some of the kabouters, both male and female, were, when they were not appointed to the first row, in which were some of the biggest of the males, and some of the fattest of the females. Then the line tapered off, to forty or fifty young folks, including urchins of either sex, down to mere babies, that could hardly stand. These had bibs on and had to be held up by their fond mothers. Each one by itself could squeal and squall, coo and crow lustily; but, at a distance, their voices blended and the noise they made sounded like a tinkle.

All being ready, the old gnome bit his tuning fork, hummed a moment, and then started a tune. Along the line, at a signal from the chief gnome, they started a tune.

In the long line, there were, at first, booms and peals, twanging and clanging, jangling and wrangling, making such a clangor that it sounded more like an uproar than an opera. The chief gnome was almost discouraged.

But neither a gnome nor a kabouter ever gives up. The master of the choir tried again and again. He scolded one old daddy, for singing too low. He frowned at a stalwart young fellow, who tried to drown out all the rest with his bull-like bellow. He shook his finger at a kabouter girl, that was flirting with a handsome lad near her. He cheered up the little folks, encouraging them to hold up their voices, until finally he had all in order. Then they practiced, until the master gnome thought he had his scale of notation perfect and gave orders to attune the bells. To the delight of all the gnomes, kabouters and elves, that had been invited to the concert, the rows of bells, a hundred or more, from boomers to tinklers, made harmony. Strung one above the other, they could render merriment, or sadness, in solos, peals, chimes, cascades and carillons, with sweetness and effect. At the low notes the babies called out "cow, cow;" but at the high notes, "bird, bird."

So it happened that, on the very day that the bishop had his great church built, with a splendid bulb spire on the top, and all nicely furnished within, but without one bell to ring in it, that the kabouters planned a great surprise.

It was night. The bishop was packing his saddle bags, ready to take a journey, on horseback, to Rheims. At this city, the great caravans from India and China ended, bringing to the annual fair, rugs, spices, gems, and things Oriental, and the merchants of Rheims rolled in gold. Here the bishop would beg the money, or ask for a bell, or chimes.

Suddenly, in the night, while in his own house, there rang out music in the air, such as the bishop had never heard in Holland, or in any of the seventeen provinces of the Netherlands. Not even in the old lands, France, or Spain, or Italy, where the Christian teachers, builders and singers, and the music of the bells had long been heard, had such a flood of sweet sounds ever fallen on human ears. Here, in these northern regions, rang out, not a solo, nor a peal, nor a chime, nor even a cascade, from one bell, or from many bells; but, a long programme of richest music in the air--something which no other country, however rich or old, possessed. It was a carillon, that is, a continued mass of real music, in which whole tunes, songs, and elaborate pieces of such length, mass and harmony, as only a choir of many voices, a band of music, or an orchestra of many performers could produce.

To get this grand work of hanging in the spire done in one night, and before daylight, also, required a whole regiment of fairy toilers, who must work like bees. For if one ray of sunshine struck any one of the kabouters, he was at once petrified. The light elves lived in the sunshine and thrived on it; but for dark elves, like the kabouters, whose home was underground, sunbeams were as poisoned arrows bringing sure death; for by these they were turned into stone. Happily the task was finished before the eastern sky grew gray, or the cocks crowed. While it was yet dark, the music in the air flooded the earth. The people in their beds listened with rapture.

"Laus Deo" (Praise God), devoutly cried the surprised bishop. "It sounds like a choir of angels. Surely the cherubim and seraphim are here. Now is fulfilled the promise of the Psalmist: 'The players on instruments shall be there.'"

So, from this beginning, so mysterious to the rough, unwise and stupid teachers, but, by degrees, clearer to the tactful ones, who were kind and patient, the carillons spread over all the region between the forests of Ardennes and the island in the North Sea. The Netherlands became the land of melodious symphonies and of tinkling bells. No town, however poor, but in time had its carillon. Every quarter of an hour, the sweet music of hymn or song, made the air vocal, while at the striking of the hours, the pious bowed their heads and the workmen heard the call for rest, or they took cheer, because their day's toil was over. At sunrise, noon, or sunset, the Angelus, and at night the curfew sounded their calls.

It grew into a fashion, that, on stated days, great concerts were given, lasting over an hour, when the grand works of the masters of music were rendered and famous carillon players came from all over the Netherlands, to compete for prizes. The Low Countries became a famous school, in which klokken-spielers (bell players) by scores were trained. Thus no kingdom, however rich or great, ever equalled the Land of the Carillon, in making the air sweet with both melody and harmony.

Nobody ever sees a kabouter nowadays, for in the new world, when the woods are nearly all cut down, the world made by the steam engine, and telegraph, and wireless message, the automobile, aeroplane and submarine, cycle and under-sea boat, the little folks in the mines and forests are forgotten. The chemists, miners, engineers and learned men possess the secrets which were once those of the fairies only. Yet the artists and architects, the clockmakers and bellfounders, who love beauty, remember what their fathers once thought and believed. That is the reason why, on many a famous clock, either in front of the dial or near the pendulum, are figures of the gnomes, who thought, and the kabouters who wrought, to make the carillons. In Teuton lands, where their cousins are named kobolds, and in France where they are called fée, and in England brownies, they have tolling and ringing of bells, with peals, chimes and cascades of sweet sound; but the Netherlands, still, above all others on earth, is the home of the carillon.

THE WOMAN WITH THREE HUNDRED AND SIXTY-SIX CHILDREN

Long, long ago, before the oldest stork was young and big deer and little fawns were very many in the Dutch forests, there was a pond, famous for its fish, which lay in the very heart of Holland, with woods near by. Hunters came with their bows and arrows to hunt the stags. Or, out of the bright waters, boys and men in the sunshine drew out the fish with shining scales, or lured the trout, with fly-bait, from their hiding places. In those days the fish-pond was called the Vijver, and the woods where the deer ran, Rensselaer, or the Deer's Lair.

So, because the forests of oak, and beech, and alder trees were so fine, and game on land and in water so plentiful, the lord of the country came here and built his castle. He made a hedge around his estate, so that the people called the place the Count's Hedge; or, as we say, The Hague. Even to-day, within the beautiful city, the forests, with their grand old trees, still remain, and the fish-pond, called the Vijver, is there yet, with its swans. On the little island, the fluffy, downy cygnets are born and grow to be big birds, with long necks, bent like an arch. In another part of the town, also, with their trees for nesting, and their pond for wading, are children of the same storks, whose fathers and mothers lived there before America was discovered.

By and by, many people of rank and fortune came to The Hague, for its society. They built their grand houses at the slope of the hill, not far away from the Vijver, and in time a city grew up.

It was a fine sight to see the lords and ladies riding out from the castle into the country. The cavalcade was very splendid, when they went hawking. There were pretty women on horseback, and gentlemen in velvet clothes, with feathers in their hats, and the horses seemed proud to bear them. The falconers followed on foot, with the hunting birds perched on a hoop, which the man inside the circle carried round him. Each falcon had on a little cap or hood, which was fastened over its head. When this was taken off, it flew high up into the air, on its hunt for the big and little birds, which it brought down for its masters. There were also men with dogs, to beat the reeds and bushes, and drive the smaller birds from shelter. The huntsmen were armed with spears, lest a wild boar, or bear, should rush out and attack them. It was always a merry day, when a hawking party, in their fine clothes and gay trappings, started out.

There were huts, as well as palaces, and poor people, also, at The Hague. Among these, was a widow, whose twin babies were left without anything to eat--for her husband and their father had been killed in the war. Having no money to buy a cradle, and her babies being too young to be left alone, she put the pair of little folks on her back and went out to beg.

Now there was a fine lady, a Countess, who lived with her husband, the Count, near the Vijver. She was childless and very jealous of other women who were mothers and had children playing around them. On this day, when the beggar woman, with her two babies on her back, came along, the grand lady was in an unusually bad temper. For all her pretty clothes, she was not a person of fine manners. Indeed, she often acted more like a snarling dog, ready to snap at any one who should speak to her. Although she had cradles and nurses and lovely baby clothes all ready, there was no baby. This spoiled her disposition, so that her husband and the servants could hardly live with her.

One day, after dinner, when there had been everything good to eat and drink on her table, and plenty of it, the Countess went out to walk in front of her house. It was the third day of January, but the weather was mild. The beggar woman, with her two babies on her back and their arms round her neck, crying with hunger, came trudging along. She went into the garden and asked the Countess for food or an alms. She expected surely, at least a slice of bread, a cup of milk, or a small coin.

But the Countess was rude to her and denied her both food and money. She even burst into a bad temper, and reviled the woman for having two children, instead of one.

"Where did you get those brats? They are not yours. You just brought them here to play on my feelings and excite my jealousy. Begone!"

But the poor woman kept her temper. She begged piteously and said: "For the love of Heaven, feed my babies, even if you will not feed me."

"No! they are not yours. You're a cheat," said the fine lady, nursing her rage.

"Indeed, Madame, they are both my children and born on one day. They have one father, but he is dead. He was killed in the war, while serving his grace, your husband."

"Don't tell me such a story," snapped back the Countess, now in a fury. "I don't believe that any one, man or woman, could have two children at once. Away with you," and she seized a stick to drive off the poor woman.

Now, it was the turn of the beggar to answer back. Both had lost their temper, and the two angry women seemed more like she-bears robbed of their whelps.

"Heaven punish you, you wicked, cruel, cold-hearted woman," cried the mother. Her two babies were almost choking her in their eagerness for food. Yet their cries never moved the rich lady, who had bread and good things to spare, while their poor parent had not a drop of milk to give them. The Countess now called her men-servants to drive the beggar away. This they did, most brutally. They pushed the poor woman outside the garden gate and closed it behind her. As she turned away, the poor mother, taking each of her children by its back, one in each hand, held them up before the grand lady and cried out loudly, so that all heard her:

"May you have as many children as there are days in the year."

Now with all her wrath burning in her breast, what the beggar woman really meant was this: It was the third of January, and so there were but three days in the year, so far. She intended to say that, instead of having to care for two children, the Countess might have the trouble of rearing three, and all born on the same day.

But the fine lady, in her mansion, cared nothing for the beggar woman's words. Why should she? She had her lordly husband, who was a count, and he owned thousands of acres. Besides, she possessed vast riches. In her great house, were ten men-servants and thirty-one maid-servants, together with her rich furniture, and fine clothes and jewels. The lofty brick church, to which she went on Sundays, was hung with the coats of arms of her famous ancestors. The stone floor, with its great slabs, was so grandly carved with the crests and heraldry of her family, that to walk over these was like climbing a mountain, or tramping across a ploughed field. Common folks had to be careful, lest they should stumble over the bosses and knobs of the carved tombs. A long train of her servants, and tenants on the farms followed her, when she went to worship. Inside the church, the lord and lady sat, in high seats, on velvet cushions and under a canopy.

By the time summer had come, according to the fashion in all good Dutch families, all sorts of pretty baby clothes were made ready. There were soft, warm, swaddling bands, tiny socks, and long white linen dresses. A baptismal blanket, covered with silk, was made for the christening, and daintily embroidered. Plenty of lace, and pink and blue ribbons--pink for a girl and blue for a boy--were kept at hand. And, because there might be twins, a double set of garments was provided, besides baby bathtubs and all sorts of nice things for the little stranger or strangers--whether one or two--to come. Even the names were chosen--one for a boy and the other for a girl. Would it be Wilhelm or Wilhelmina?

It was real fun to think over the names, but it was hard to choose out of so many. At last, the Countess crossed off all but forty-six; or the following; nearly every girl's name ending in *je*, as in our "Polly," "Sallie."

Girls		*Boys*	
Magtel	Catharyna	Gerrit	Gysbert
Nelletje	Alida	Cornelis	Jausze
Zelia	Annatje	Volkert	Myndert
Jannetje	Christina	Kilian	Adrian
Zara	Katrina	Johannes	Joachim
Marytje	Bethje	Petrus	Arendt
Willemtje	Eva	Barent	Dirck
Geertruy	Dirkje	Wessel	Nikolaas
Petronella	Mayken	Hendrik	Staats
Margrieta	Hilleke	Teunis	Gozen
Josina	Bethy	Wouter	Willemtje
	Japik	Evert	

But before the sun set on the expected day, it was neither one boy nor one girl, nor both; nor were all the forty-six names chosen sufficient; for the beggar woman's wish had come true, in a way not expected. There were as many as, and no fewer children than, there were days in the year; and, since this was leap year, there were three hundred and sixty-six little folks in the house; so that other names, besides the forty-six, had to be used.

Yet none of these wee creatures was bigger than a mouse. Beginning at daylight, one after another appeared--first a girl and then a boy; so that after the forty-eighth, the nurse was at her wit's end, to give them names. It was not possible to keep the little babies apart. The thirty-one servant maids of the mansion were all called in to help in sorting out the girls from the boys; but soon it seemed hopeless to try to pick out Peter from Henry, or Catalina from Annetje. After an hour or two spent at the task, and others coming along, the women found that it was useless to try any longer. It was found that little Piet, Jan and Klaas, Hank, Douw and Japik, among the boys; and Molly, Mayka, Lena, Elsje, Annatje and Marie were getting all mixed up. So they gave up the attempt in despair. Besides, the supply of pink and blue ribbons had given out long before, after the first dozen or so were born. As for the baby clothes made ready, they were of no use, for all the garments were too big. In one of the long dresses, tied up like a bag, one might possibly, with stuffing, have put the whole family of three hundred and sixty-six brothers and sisters.

It was not likely such small fry of human beings could live long. So, the good Bishop Guy, of Utrecht, when he heard that the beggar woman's curse had come true, in so unexpected a manner, ordered that the babies should be all baptized at once. The Count, who was strict in his ideas of both custom and church law, insisted on it too.

So nothing would do but to carry the tiny infants to church. How to get them there, was a question. The whole house had been rummaged to provide things to carry the little folks in: but the supply of trays, and mince pie dishes, and crocks, was exhausted at the three hundred and sixtieth baby. So there was left only a Turk's Head, or round glazed earthen dish, fluted and curved, which looked like the turban of a Turk. Hence its name. Into this, the last batch of babies, or extra six girls, were stowed. Curiously enough, number 366 was an inch taller than the others. To thirty house maids was given a tray, for each was to carry twelve mannikins, and one the last six, in the Turk's Head. Instead of rich silk blankets a wooden tray, and no clothes on, must suffice.

In the Groote Kerk, or Great Church, the Bishop was waiting, with his assistants, holding brass basins full of holy water, for the christening. All the town, including the dogs, were out to see what was going on. Many boys and girls climbed up on the roofs of the one-story houses, or in the trees to get a better view of the curious procession--the like of which had never been seen in The Hague before. Neither has anything like it ever been seen since.

So the parade began. First went the Count, with his captains and the trumpeters, blowing their trumpets. These were followed by the men-servants, all dressed in their best Sunday clothes, who had the crest and arms of their master, the Count, on their backs and breasts. Then came on the company of thirty-one maids, each one carrying a tray, on which were twelve mannikins, or minikins. Twenty of these trays were round and made of wood, lined with velvet, smooth and soft; but ten were of earthenware, oblong in shape, like a manger. In these, every year, were baked the Christmas pies.

At first, all went on finely, for the outdoor air seemed to put the babies asleep and there was no crying. But no sooner were they inside the church, than about two hundred of the brats began wailing and whimpering. Pretty soon, they set up such a squall that the Count felt ashamed of his progeny and the Bishop looked very unhappy.

To make matters worse, one of the maids, although warned of the danger, stumbled over the helmet of an old crusader, carved in stone, that rose some six inches or so above the floor. In a moment, she fell and lay sprawling, spilling out at least a dozen babies. "Heilige Mayke" (Holy Mary!), she cried, as she rolled over. "Have I killed them?"

Happily the wee ones were thrown against the long-trained gown of an old lady walking directly in front of her, so that they were unhurt. They were easily picked up and laid on the tray again, and once more the line started.

Happily the Bishop had been notified that he would not have to call out the names of all the infants, that is, three hundred and sixty-six; for this would have kept him at the solemn business all day long. It had been arranged that, instead of any on the list of the chosen forty-six, to be so named, all the boys should be called John, and all the girls Elizabeth; or, in Dutch, Jan and Lisbet, or Lizbethje. Yet even to say "John" one hundred and eighty times, and "Lisbet" one hundred and eighty-six times, nearly tired the old gentleman to death, for he was fat and slow.

So, after the first six trays full of wee folks had been sprinkled, one at a time, the Bishop decided to "asperse" them, that is, shake, from a mop or brush, the holy water, on a tray full of babies at one time. So he called for the "aspersorium." Then, clipping this in the basin of holy water, he scattered the drops over the wee folk, until all, even the six extra girl babies in the Turk's Head, were sprinkled. Probably, because the Bishop thought a Turk was next door to a heathen, he dropped more water than usual on these last six, until the young ones squealed lustily with the cold. It was noted, on the contrary, that the little folks in the mince pie dishes were gently handled, as if the good man had visions of Christmas coming and the good things on the table.

Yet it was evident that such tiny people could not bear what healthy babies of full size would think nothing of. Whether it was because of the damp weather, or the cold air in the brick church, or too much excitement, or because there were not three hundred and sixty-six nurses, or milk bottles ready, it came to pass that every one of the wee creatures died when the sun went down.

Just where they were buried is not told, but, for hundreds of years, there was, in one of The Hague churches, a monument in honor of these little folks, who lived but a day. It was graven with portraits in stone of the Count and Countess and told of their children, as many as the days of the year. Near by, were hung up the two basins, in which the holy water, used by the Bishop, in sprinkling the babies, was held. The year, month and day of the wonderful event were also engraved. Many and many people from various lands came to visit the tomb. The guide books spoke of it, and tender women wept, as they thought how three hundred and sixty-six little cradles, in the Count's castle, would have looked, had each baby lived.

THE ONI ON HIS TRAVELS

Across the ocean, in Japan, there once lived curious creatures called Onis. Every Japanese boy and girl has heard of them, though one has not often been caught. In one museum, visitors could see the hairy leg of a specimen. Falling out of the air in a storm, the imp had lost his limb. It had been torn off by being caught in the timber side of a well curb. The story-teller was earnestly assured by one Japanese lad that his grandfather had seen it tumble from the clouds.

Many people are sure that the Onis live in the clouds and occasionally fall off, during a peal of thunder. Then they escape and hide down in a well. Or, they get loose in the kitchen, rattle the dishes around, and make a great racket. They behave like cats, with a dog after them. They do a great deal of mischief, but not much harm. There are even some old folks who say that, after all, Onis are only unruly children, that behave like angels in the morning and act like imps in the afternoon. So we see that not much is known about the Onis.

Many things that go wrong are blamed on the Onis. Foolish folks, such as stupid maid-servants, and dull-witted fellows, that blunder a good deal, declare that the Onis made them do it. Drunken men, especially, that stumble into mud-holes at night, say the Onis pushed them in. Naughty boys that steal cake, and girls that take sugar, often tell fibs to their parents, charging it on the Onis.

The Onis love to play jokes on people, but they are not dangerous. There are plenty of pictures of them in Japan, though they never sat for their portraits, but this is the way they looked.

Some Onis have only one eye in their forehead, others two, and, once in a while, a big fellow has three. There are little, short horns on their heads, but these are no bigger than those on a baby deer and never grow long. The hair on their heads gets all snarled up, just like a little girl's that cries when her tangled tresses are combed out; for the Onis make use of neither brushes nor looking glasses. As for their faces, they never wash them, so they look sooty. Their skin is rough, like an elephant's. On each of their feet are only three toes. Whether an Oni has a nose, or a snout, is not agreed upon by the learned men who have studied them.

No one ever heard of an Oni being higher than a yardstick, but they are so strong that one of them can easily lift two bushel bags of rice at once. In Japan, they steal the food offered to the idols. They can live without air. They like nothing better than to drink both the rice spirit called saké, and the black liquid called soy, of which only a few drops, as a sauce on fish, are enough for a man. Of this sauce, the Dutch, as well as the Japanese, are very fond.

Above all things else, the most fun for a young Oni is to get into a crockery shop. Once there, he jumps round among the cups and dishes, hides in the jars, straddles the shelves and turns somersaults over the counter. In fact, the Oni is only a jolly little imp. The Japanese girls, on New Year's eve, throw handfuls of dried beans in every room of the house and cry, "In, with good luck; and out with you, Onis!" Yet they laugh merrily all the time. The Onis cannot speak, but they can chatter like monkeys. They often seem to be talking to each other in gibberish.

Now it once happened in Japan that the great Tycoon of the country wanted to make a present to the Prince of the Dutch. So he sent all over the land, from the sweet potato fields in the south to the seal and salmon waters in the north, to get curiosities of all sorts. The products of Japan, from the warm parts, where grow the indigo and the sugar cane, to the cold regions, in which are the bear and walrus, were sent as gifts to go to the Land of Dykes and Windmills. The Japanese had heard that the Dutch people like cheese, walk in wooden shoes, eat with forks, instead of chopsticks, and the women wear twenty petticoats apiece, while the men sport jackets with two gold buttons, and folks generally do things the other way from that which was common in Japan.

Now it chanced that while they were packing the things that were piled up in the palace at Yedo, a young Oni, with his horns only half grown, crawled into the kitchen, at night, through the big bamboo water pipe near the pump. Pretty soon he jumped into the storeroom. There, the precious cups, vases, lacquer boxes, pearl-inlaid pill-holders, writing desks, jars of tea, and bales of silk, were lying about, ready to be put into their cases. The yellow wrappings for covering the pretty things of gold and silver, bronze and wood, and the rice chaff, for the packing of the porcelain, were all at hand. What a jolly time the Oni did have, in tumbling them about and rolling over them! Then he leaped like a monkey from one vase to another. He put on a lady's gay silk kimono and wrapped himself around with golden embroidery. Then he danced and played the game of the Ka-gu'-ra, or Lion of Korea, pretending to make love to a girl-Oni. Such funny capers as he did cut! It would have made a cat laugh to see him. It was broad daylight, before his pranks were over, and the Dutch church chimes were playing the hour of seven.

Suddenly the sound of keys in the lock told him that, in less than a minute, the door would open.

Where should he hide? There was no time to be lost. So he seized some bottles of soy from the kitchen shelf and then jumped into the big bottom drawer of a ladies' cabinet, and pulled it shut.

"Namu Amida" (Holy Buddha!), cried the man that opened the door. "Who has been here? It looks like a rat's picnic."

However, the workmen soon came and set everything to rights. Then they packed up the pretty things. They hammered down the box lids and before night the Japanese curiosities were all stored in the hold of a swift, Dutch ship, from Nagasaki, bound for Rotterdam. After a long voyage, the vessel arrived safely in good season, and the boxes were sent on to The Hague, or capital city. As the presents were for the Prince, they were taken at once to the pretty palace, called the House in the Wood. There they were unpacked and set on exhibition for the Prince and Princess to see the next day.

When the palace maid came in next morning to clean up the floor and dust the various articles, her curiosity led her to pull open the drawer of the ladies' cabinet; when out jumped something hairy. It nearly frightened the girl out of her wits. It was the Oni, which rushed off and down stairs, tumbling over a half dozen servants, who were sitting at their breakfast. All started to run except the brave butler, who caught up a carving knife and showed fight. Seeing this, the Oni ran down into the cellar, hoping to find some hole or crevice for escape. All around, were shelves filled with cheeses, jars of sour-krout, pickled herring, and stacks of fresh rye bread standing in the corners. But oh! how they did smell in his Japanese nostrils! Oni, as he was, he nearly fainted, for no such odors had ever beaten upon his nose, when in Japan. Even at the risk of being carved into bits, he must go back. So up into the kitchen again he ran. Happily, the door into the garden stood wide open.

Grabbing a fresh bottle of soy from the kitchen shelf, the Oni, with a hop, skip and jump, reached outdoors. Seeing a pair of klomps, or wooden shoes, near the steps, the Oni put his pair of three toes into them, to keep the dogs from scenting its tracks. Then he ran into the fields, hiding among the cows, until he heard men with pitchforks coming. At once the Oni leaped upon a cow's back and held on to its horns, while the poor animal ran for its life into its stall, in the cow stable, hoping to brush the monster off.

The dairy farmer's wife was at that moment pulling open her bureau drawer, to put on a new clean lace cap. Hearing her favorite cow moo and bellow, she left the drawer open and ran to look through the pane of glass in the kitchen. Through this, she could peep, at any minute, to see whether this or that cow, or its calf, was sick or well.

Meanwhile, at the House in the Wood, the Princess, hearing the maid scream and the servants in an uproar, rushed out in her embroidered white nightie, to ask who, and what, and why, and wherefore. All different and very funny were the answers of maid, butler, cook, valet and boots.

The first maid, who had pulled open the drawer and let the Oni get out, held up broom and duster, as if to take oath. She declared:

"It was a monkey, or baboon; but he seemed to talk--Russian, I think."

"No," said the butler. "I heard the creature--a black ram, running on its hind legs; but its language was German, I'm sure."

The cook, a fat Dutch woman, told a long story. She declared, on honor, that it was a black dog like a Chinese pug, that has no hair. However, she had only seen its back, but she was positive the creature talked English, for she heard it say "soy."

The valet honestly avowed that he was too scared to be certain of anything, but was ready to swear that to his ears the words uttered seemed to be Swedish. He had once heard sailors from Sweden talking, and the chatter sounded like their lingo.

Then there was Boots, the errand boy, who believed that it was the Devil; but, whatever or whoever it was, he was ready to bet a week's wages that its lingo was all in French.

Now when the Princess found that not one of her servants could speak or understand any language but their own, she scolded them roundly in Dutch, and wound up by saying, "You're a lot of cheese-heads, all of you."

Then she arranged the wonderful things from the Far East, with her own dainty hands, until the House in the Wood was fragrant with Oriental odors, and soon it became famous throughout all Europe. Even when her grandchildren played with the pretty toys from the land of Fuji and flowers, of silk and tea, cherry blossoms and camphor trees, it was not only the first but the finest Japanese collection in all Europe.

Meanwhile, the Oni, in a strange land, got into one trouble after another. In rushed men with clubs, but as an Oni was well used to seeing these at home, he was not afraid. He could outrun, outjump, or outclimb any man, easily. The farmer's vrouw (wife) nearly fainted when the Oni leaped first into her room and then into her bureau drawer. As he did so, the bottle of soy, held in his three-fingered paw, hit the wood and the dark liquid, as black as tar, ran all over the nicely starched laces, collars and nightcaps. Every bit of her quilled and crimped hear-gear and neckwear, once as white as snow, was ruined.

"Donder en Bliksem" (thunder and lightning), cried the vrouw. "There's my best cap, that cost twenty guilders, utterly ruined." Then she bravely ran for the broomstick.

The Oni caught sight of what he thought was a big hole in the wall and ran into it. Seeing the blue sky above, he began to climb up. Now there were no chimneys in Japan and he did not know what this was. The soot nearly blinded and choked him. So he slid down and rushed out, only to have his head nearly cracked by the farmer's wife, who gave him a whack of her broomstick. She thought it was a crazy goat that she was fighting. She first drove the Oni into the cellar and then bolted the door.

An hour later, the farmer got a gun and loaded it. Then, with his hired man he came near, one to pull open the door, and the other to shoot. What they expected to find was a monster.

But no! So much experience, even within an hour, of things unknown in Japan, including chimneys, had been too severe for the poor, lonely, homesick Oni. There it lay dead on the floor, with its three fingers held tightly to its snout and closing it. So much cheese, zuur kool (sour krout), gin (schnapps), advocaat (brandy and eggs), cows' milk, both sour and fresh, wooden shoes, lace collars and crimped neckwear, with the various smells, had turned both the Oni's head and his stomach. The very sight of these strange things being so unusual, gave the Oni first fright, and then a nervous attack, while the odors, such as had never tortured his nose before, had finished him.

The wise men of the village were called together to hold an inquest. After summoning witnesses, and cross-examining them and studying the strange creature, their verdict was that it could be nothing less than a *Hersen Schim*, that is, a spectre of the brain. They meant by this that there was no such animal.

However, a man from Delft, who followed the business of a knickerbocker, or baker of knickers, or clay marles, begged the body of the Oni. He wanted it to serve as a model for a new gargoyle, or rain spout, for the roof of churches. Carved in stone, or baked in clay, which turns red and is called terra cotta, the new style of monster became very popular. The knickerbocker named it after a new devil, that had been expelled by the prayers of the saints, and speedily made a fortune, by selling it to stone cutters and architects. So for one real Oni, that died and was buried in Dutch soil, there are thousands of imaginary ones, made of baked clay, or stone, in the Dutch land, where things, more funny than in fairy-land, constantly take place.

The dead Japanese Oni serving as a model, which was made into a water gutter, served more useful purposes, for a thousand years, than ever he had done, in the land where his relations still live and play their pranks.

THE LEGEND OF THE WOODEN SHOE

In years long gone, too many for the almanac to tell of, or for clocks and watches to measure, millions of good fairies came down from the sun and went into the earth. There, they changed themselves into roots and leaves, and became trees. There were many kinds of these, as they covered the earth, but the pine and birch, ash and oak, were the chief ones that made Holland. The fairies that lived in the trees bore the name of Moss Maidens, or Tree "Trintjes," which is the Dutch pet name for Kate, or Katharine.

The oak was the favorite tree, for people lived then on acorns, which they ate roasted, boiled or mashed, or made into meal, from which something like bread was kneaded and baked. With oak bark, men tanned hides and made leather, and, from its timber, boats and houses. Under its branches, near the trunk, people laid their sick, hoping for help from the gods. Beneath the oak boughs, also, warriors took oaths to be faithful to their lords, women made promises, or wives joined hand in hand around its girth, hoping to have beautiful children. Up among its leafy branches the new babies lay, before they were found in the cradle by the other children. To make a young child grow up to be strong and healthy, mothers drew them through a split sapling or young tree. Even more wonderful, as medicine for the country itself, the oak had power to heal. The new land sometimes suffered from disease called the *val* (or fall). When sick with the *val*, the ground sunk. Then people, houses, churches, barns and cattle all went down, out of sight, and were lost forever, in a flood of water.

But the oak, with its mighty roots, held the soil firm. Stories of dead cities, that had tumbled beneath the waves, and of the famous Forest of Reeds, covering a hundred villages, which disappeared in one night, were known only too well.

Under the birch tree, lovers met to plight their vows, and on its smooth bark was often cut the figure of two hearts joined in one. In summer, the forest furnished shade, and in winter warmth from the fire. In the spring time, the new leaves were a wonder, and in autumn the pigs grew fat on the mast, or the acorns, that had dropped on the ground.

So, for thousands of years, when men made their home in the forest, and wanted nothing else, the trees were sacred.

But by and by, when cows came into the land and sheep and horses multiplied, more open ground was needed for pasture, grain fields and meadows. Fruit trees, bearing apples and pears, peaches and cherries, were planted, and grass, wheat, rye and barley were grown. Then, instead of the dark woods, men liked to have their gardens and orchards open to the sunlight. Still, the people were very rude, and all they had on their bare feet were rough bits of hard leather, tied on through their toes; though most of them went barefooted.

The forests had to be cut down. Men were so busy with the axe, that in a few years, the Wood Land was gone. Then the new "Holland," with its people and red roofed houses, with its chimneys and windmills, and dykes and storks, took the place of the old Holt Land of many trees.

Now there was a good man, a carpenter and very skilful with his tools, who so loved the oak that he gave himself, and his children after him, the name of Eyck, which is pronounced Ike, and is Dutch for oak. When, before his neighbors and friends, according to the beautiful Dutch custom, he called his youngest born child, to lay the corner-stone of his new house, he bestowed upon her, before them all, the name of Neeltje (or Nellie) Van Eyck.

The carpenter daddy continued to mourn over the loss of the forests. He even shed tears, fearing lest, by and by, there should not one oak tree be left in the country. Moreover, he was frightened at the thought that the new land, made by pushing back the ocean and building dykes, might sink down again and go back to the fishes. In such a case, all the people, the babies and their mothers, men, women, horses and cattle, would be drowned. The Dutch folks were a little too fast, he thought, in winning their acres from the sea.

One day, while sitting on his door-step, brooding sorrowfully, a Moss Maiden and a Tree Elf appeared, skipping along, hand in hand. They came up to him and told him that his ancestral oak had a message for him. Then they laughed and ran away. Van Eyck, which was now the man's full family name, went into the forest and stood under the grand old oak tree, which his fathers loved, and which he would allow none to cut down.

Looking up, the leaves of the tree rustled, and one big branch seemed to sweep near him. Then it whispered in his ear:

"Do not mourn, for your descendants, even many generations hence, shall see greater things than you have witnessed. I and my fellow oak trees shall pass away, but the sunshine shall be spread over the land and make it dry. Then, instead of its falling down, like acorns from the trees, more and better food shall come up from out of the earth. Where green fields now spread, and the cities grow where forests were, we shall come to life again, but in another form. When most needed, we shall furnish you and your children and children's children, with warmth, comfort, fire, light, and wealth. Nor need you fear for the land, that it will fall; for, even while living, we, and all the oak trees that are left, and all the birch, beech, and pine trees shall stand on our heads for you. We shall hold up your houses, lest they fall into the ooze and you shall walk and run over our heads. As truly as when rooted in the soil, will we do this. Believe what we tell you, and be happy. We shall turn ourselves upside down for you."

"I cannot see how all these things can be," said Van Eyck.

"Fear not, my promise will endure."

The leaves of the branch rustled for another moment. Then, all was still, until the Moss Maiden and Trintje, the Tree Elf, again, hand in hand, as they tripped along merrily, appeared to him. "We shall help you and get our friends, the elves, to do the same. Now, do you take some oak wood and saw off two pieces, each a foot long. See that they are well dried. Then set them on the kitchen table to-night, when you go to bed." After saying this, and looking at each other and laughing, just as girls do, they disappeared.

Pondering on what all this might mean, Van Eyck went to his wood-shed and sawed off the oak timber. At night, after his wife had cleared off the supper table, he laid the foot-long pieces in their place.

When Van Eyck woke up in the morning, he recalled his dream, and, before he was dressed, hurried to the kitchen. There, on the table, lay a pair of neatly made wooden shoes. Not a sign of tools, or shavings could be seen, but the clean wood and pleasant odor made him glad. When he glanced again at the wooden shoes, he found them perfectly smooth, both inside and out. They had heels at the bottom and were nicely pointed at the toes, and, altogether, were very inviting to the foot. He tried them on, and found that they fitted him exactly. He tried to walk on the kitchen floor, which his wife kept scrubbed and polished, and then sprinkled with clean white sand, with broomstick ripples scored in the layers, but for Van Eyck it was like walking on ice. After slipping and balancing himself, as if on a tight rope, and nearly breaking his nose against the wall, he took off the wooden shoes, and kept them off, while inside the house. However, when he went outdoors, he found his new shoes very light, pleasant to the feet and easy to walk in. It was not so much like trying to skate, as it had been in the kitchen.

At night, in his dreams, he saw two elves come through the window into the kitchen. One, a kabouter, dark and ugly, had a box of tools. The other, a light-faced elf, seemed to be the guide. The kabouter at once got out his saw, hatchet, auger, long, chisel-like knife, and smoothing plane. At first, the two elves seemed to be quarrelling, as to who should be boss. Then they settled down quietly to work. The kabouter took the wood and shaped it on the outside. Then he hollowed out, from inside of it, a pair of shoes, which the elf smoothed and polished. Then one elf put his little feet in them and tried to dance, but he only slipped on the smooth floor and flattened his nose; but the other fellow pulled the nose straight again, so it was all right. They waltzed together upon the wooden shoes, then took them off, jumped out the window, and ran away.

When Van Eyck put the wooden shoes on, he found that out in the fields, in the mud, and on the soft soil, and in sloppy places, this sort of foot gear was just the thing. They did not sink in the mud and the man's feet were comfortable, even after hours of labor. They did not "draw" his feet, and they kept out the water far better than leather possibly could.

When the Van Eyck vrouw and the children saw how happy Daddy was, they each one wanted a pair. Then they asked him what he called them.

"Klompen," said he, in good Dutch, and klompen, or klomps, they are to this day.

"I'll make a fortune out of this," said Van Eyck. "I'll set up a klomp-winkel (shop for wooden shoes) at once."

So, going out to the blacksmith's shop, in the village, he had the man who pounded iron fashion for him on his anvil, a set of tools, exactly like those used by the kabouter and the elf, which he had seen in his dream. Then he hung out a sign, marked "Wooden blocks for shoes." He made klomps for the little folks just out of the nursery, for boys and girls, for grown men and women, and for all who walked out-of-doors, in the street or on the fields.

Soon klomps came to be the fashion in all the country places. It was good manners, when you went into a house, to take off your wooden shoes and leave them at the door. Even in the towns and cities, ladies wore wooden slippers, especially when walking or working in the garden.

Klomps also set the fashion for soft, warm socks, and stockings made from sheep's wool. Soon, a thousand needles were clicking, to put a soft cushion between one's soles and toes and the wood. Women knitted, even while they walked to market, or gossiped on the streets. The klomp-winkels, or shops of the shoe carpenters, were seen in every village.

When rich beyond his day-dreams, Van Eyck had another joyful night vision. The next day, he wore a smiling countenance. Everybody, who met him on the street, saluted him and asked, in a neighborly way:

"Good-morning, Mynheer Bly-moe-dig (Mr. Cheerful). How do you sail to-day?"

That's the way the Dutch talk--not "how do you do," but, in their watery country, it is this, "How do you sail?" or else, "Hoe gat het u al?" (How goes it with you, already?)

Then Van Eyck told his dream. It was this: The Moss Maiden and Trintje, the wood elf, came to him again at night and danced. They were lively and happy.

"What now?" asked the dreamer, smilingly, of his two visitors.

He had hardly got the question out of his mouth, when in walked a kabouter, all smutty with blacksmith work. In one hand, he grasped his tool box. In the other, he held a curious looking machine. It was a big lump of iron, set in a frame, with ropes to pull it up and let it fall down with a thump.

"What is it?" asked Van Eyck.

"It's a Hey" (a pile driver), said the kabouter, showing him how to use it. "When men say to you, on the street, to-morrow, 'How do you sail?' laugh at them," said the Moss Maiden, herself laughing.

"Yes, and now you can tell the people how to build cities, with mighty churches with lofty towers, and with high houses like those in other lands. Take the trees, trim the branches off, sharpen the tops, turn them upside down and pound them deep in the ground. Did not the ancient oak promise that the trees would be turned upside down for you? Did they not say you could walk on top of them?"

By this time, Van Eyck had asked so many questions, and kept the elves so long, that the Moss Maiden peeped anxiously through the window. Seeing the day breaking, she and Trintje and the kabouter flew away, so as not to be petrified by the sunrise.

"I'll make another fortune out of this, also," said the happy man, who, next morning, was saluted as Mynheer Blyd-schap (Mr. Joyful).

At once, Van Eyck set up a factory for making pile drivers. Sending men into the woods, who chose the tall, straight trees, he had their branches cut off. Then he sharpened the trunks at one end, and these were driven, by the pile driver, down, far and deep, into the ground. So a foundation, as good as stone, was made in the soft and spongy soil, and well built houses uprose by the thousands. Even the lofty walls of churches stood firm. The spires were unshaken in the storm.

Old Holland had not fertile soil like France, or vast flocks of sheep, producing wool, like England, or armies of weavers, as in the Belgic lands. Yet, soon there rose large cities, with splendid mansions and town halls. As high towards heaven as the cathedrals and towers in other lands, which had rock for foundation, her brick churches rose in the air. On top of the forest trees, driven deep into the sand and clay, dams and dykes were built, that kept out the ocean. So, instead of the old two thousand square miles, there were, in the realm, in the course of years, twelve thousand, rich in green fields and cattle. Then, for all the boys and girls that travel in this land of quaint customs, Holland was a delight.

THE CURLY-TAILED LION

Once upon a time, some Dutch hunters went to Africa, hoping to capture a whole family of lions. In this they succeeded. With a pack of hounds and plenty of aborigines to poke the jungle with sticks, they drove a big male lion, with his wife and four whelps, out of the undergrowth into a circle. In the centre, they had dug a pit and covered it over with sticks and grass. Into this, the whole lion family tumbled. Then, by nets and ropes, the big, fierce creatures and the little cubs were lifted out. They were put in cages and brought to Holland. The baby lions, no bigger than pug dogs, were as pretty and harmless as kittens. The sailors delighted to play with them.

Now lions, even before one was ever seen among the Dutch, enjoyed a great reputation for strength, courage, dignity and power. It was believed that they had all the traits of character supposed to belong to kings, and which boys like to possess. Many fathers had named their sons Leo, which is Latin for lion. Dutch daddies had their baby boys christened with the name of Leeuw, which is their word for the king of beasts.

Before lions were brought from the hot countries into colder lands, the bear and wolf were most admired; because, besides possessing plenty of fur, as well as great claws and terrible teeth, they had great courage. For these reasons, many royal and common folks had taken the wolf and bear as namesakes for their hopeful sons.

But the male lion could make more noise than wolves, for he could roar, while they could only howl. He had a shaggy mane and a very long tail. This had a nail at the end, for scratching and combing out his hair, when tangled up. If he were angry, the mighty brute could stick out his red tongue, curled like a pump handle, and nearly half a yard long.

So the lion was called the king of beasts, and the crowned rulers and knights took him as their emblem. They had pictures of the huge creature painted on their flags, shields and armor. Sometimes they stuck a gold or brass lion on their iron war hats, which they called helmets. No knight was allowed to have more than one lion on his shield, but kings might have three or four, or even a whole menagerie of meat-eating creatures. These painted or sculptured lions were in all sorts of action, running, walking, standing up and looking behind or before.

Now there was a Dutch artist, who noticed what funny fellows kings were, and how they liked to have all sorts of beasts and birds of prey, and sea creatures that devour, on their banners. There were dragons, two-headed eagles, boars with tusks, serpents with fangs, hawks, griffins, wyverns, lions, dragons and dragon-lions, besides horses with wings, mermaids with scaly tails, and even night mares that went flying through the dark. With such a funny variety of beast, bird, and fish, some wondered why there were not cows with two tails, cats with two noses, rams with four horns, and creatures that were half veal and half mutton. He noticed that kings did not care much for tame, quiet, peaceable, or useful creatures, such as oxen or horses, doves or sheep; but only for those brutes that hunt and kill the more defenceless creatures.

Since, then, kings of the country must have a lion, the artist resolved to make a new one. He would have some fun, at any rate.

So as painter or sculptor select men and women to pose for them in their study as their heroes and heroines, and just as they picture plump little boys and girls as cherubs and angels, so the Dutchman would make of the cubs and the father beast of prey his models for coats of arms.

Poor lions! They did not know, but they soon found out how tiresome it was to pose. They must hold their paws up, down, sideways or behind, according as they were told. They must stand or kneel, for a long time, in awkward positions. They must stick out their tongues to full length, walk on their hind legs, twist their necks, to one side or the other, look forward or backward, and in many tiresome ways do just as they were ordered. They must also make of their tails every sort of use, whether to wrap around posts or bundles, to stick out of their cage, or put between their legs, as they ran away, or to whisk them around, as they roared; or hoist them up high when rampant.

In some cases, they were expected, even, to put on spectacles, and pretend to be reading, to hold in their paws books and scrolls, or town arms, or shop signs. They must pose, not only as companions of Daniel, in the lions' den at Babylon, which was proper; but also to sit, as companion of St. Mark, and even to stand on their legs on the top of a high column, without falling off.

In a word, this artist belonged to the college of heralds, and he introduced the king of beasts into Dutch heraldry.

So from that day forth, the life of that family of African lions, from the daddy to the youngest cub, was made a burden. When at home in the jungle and even in the cage, the father lion's favorite position was that of lolling on one side, with his paws stretched out, and half asleep and all day, until he went out, towards dark, to hunt. Now, he must stand up, nearly all day. Daddy lion had to do most of the posing, until the poor beast's front legs and paws were weary with standing so long. Moreover, the hair was all worn off his body at the place where he had to sit on the hard wooden floor. He must do all this, on penalty of being punched with a red hot poker, if he refused. A charcoal furnace and long andirons were kept near by, and these were attended to by a Dutch boy. Or, it might be that the whole family of lions were not allowed to have any dinner till Daddy obeyed and did what he was told, though often with a snarl or a roar.

First, Leo must rise upon his hind legs and look in front of him. This posture was not hard, for in his native jungle, he had often thus obtained a breakfast of venison for his wife and family. But oh, to stand a half hour on two legs only, when he had four, and would gladly have used all of them, was hard. Yet this was the position, called "the lion rampant," which kings liked best.

But the king's uncles, nephews, nieces, cousins, and his wife's relations generally, every one of them, wanted a lion on his or her stationery and pocket handkerchiefs, as well as on their shields and flags. So the old lion was tortured--the hot poker being always in sight--and he was made to take a great variety of positions. The artist called out to Leo, just as a driver says to his cart horse, "whoa," "get up," "golong," etc. When he yelled in this fashion, the lion had to obey.

Pretty soon lions in heraldry, on flags, armor, town arms, family crests and city seals became all the fashion. The whole country went lion-mad. There were lions carved in stone, wood and iron, and every sort and kind, possible or impossible. Some of them seemed to be engaged in a variety of tricks, as if they belonged to a circus, or were having a holiday. They laughed, giggled, yawned, stuck out their tongues, held boards for hotels, bundles for the shopkeepers, or barrels for beer halls, and made excellent shop signs, which the boys and girls enjoyed looking at.

Mrs. Leo was not in much demand, for Mr. Leo did not approve of his wife's appearing in public. She was kept busy in taking care of her cubs. Daddy Lion had to do multiple work for his family, until the cubs were grown. Yet long before this time had come, their Dad had died and been stuffed for a museum. How this first king of beasts in the Netherlands came to his untimely end was on this wise.

Not satisfied with posing Leo in every posture, and with all possible gestures, his master, the artist, wanted him to look "heraldical"; that is, like some of the mythical beasts that were combinations of any and all creatures having fins, fur, feathers, or scales, such as the dragon or griffin. One day, he attempted to make out of a live lion a fanciful creature of curlicues and curliewurlies. So he strapped the lion down, and used a curling iron on his mane until he looked like a bearded bull of Babylon. Then he combed out, and, with curl papers, twisted the long line of hair, which is seen in front of Leo's stomach. In like manner, he treated the bunches of hair that grow over the animal's kneepans and elbows. Last of all, he took a hair brush, and smoothed out the tuft, at the end of the animal's long tail. Then the artist made a picture of him in this condition, all curled and rich in ringlets, like a dandy.

By this time, the father of the lion family looked as if he had come out fresh from a hairdresser's parlor. Indeed, Mrs. Leo was so struck with her husband's appearance, that she immediately licked her cubs all over, until their fur shone, so they should look like their father. Then, having used her tongue as a comb, to make her own skin smooth and glossy, she completed the job by using the nail in her tail, to do the finishing work. Altogether, this was the curliest family of lions ever seen, and Daddy Leo appeared to be the funniest curly-headed and curly-bodied lion ever seen. In fact he was all curls, from head to tail.

Notwithstanding all his pains, the artist was not yet satisfied with his job. He wanted a circle of long hair to grow in the middle of the lion's tail. His curly lion should beat all creation, and in this way he proceeded.

His own daughter, being a young lady and having some trouble of the throat, the doctor had ordered medicine for the girl, charging her not to spill any drops of the liquid on her face, or clothes.

But, in giving the dose, either the mother, or the daughter, was careless. At that very moment the cat ran across the room, after the mouse, and just as she held the spoon to her mouth, Puss got twisted in her skirts. So most of the medicine splashed upon her upper lip and then ran down to her chin, on either side of her mouth. She laughed over the spill, wiped off the liquid, and thought no more of the matter.

But a week later, she was astonished. On waking, she looked in the glass, only to shrink back in horror. On her face had grown both moustaches and a beard. True, both were rather downy, but still they were black; and, until the barber came, and shaved off the growth, she was a bearded woman. Yet, strange to tell, after one or two shaves by the barber, no more hair grew again on her face, which was smooth again.

"By Saint Servatus! I'll make a fortune on this," cried the artist, when he saw his daughter's hairy face.

So, he sold his secret to a druggist, and this man made an ointment, giving it a Chinese name, meaning "beard-grower." This wonderful medicine, as his sign declared, would "force the growth of luxuriant moustaches and a beard, on the smoothest face of any young man," who should buy and apply it.

Soon the whole town rang with the news of the wonderful discovery. The druggist sold out his stock, in two days, to happy purchasers. Other young fellows, that wanted to outrival their companions, had to wait a fortnight for the new medicine to be made. By that time, a full crop of downy hair had come out on the cheeks and chin and upper lip of many a youth. Some, who had been trying for years to raise moustaches, in order duly to impress the girls, to whom they were making love, were now jubilant. In several cases, a lover was able to cut out his rival and win the maid he wanted. Several courtings were hastened and became genuine matches, because a face, long very smooth, and like a desert as to hair, bore a promising crop. Beard and cheeks had at last met together. So the new medicine was called a "match-maker."

The artist rubbed his hands in glee, at the prospect of a fortune. He argued that if the wonderful ointment made beards for men, it must be good for lions also. So again, Daddy Lion was coerced by the threat of the hot poker. Then his tail was seized, and, by means of a rope, tied to a post on one side of the cage, he was held fast. Then the artist anointed about six inches of the middle of the smooth tail with the magic liquid. For fear the lion might lick it off, the poor beast was held in this tiresome position for a whole week, so that he could not turn round, and he nearly died of fatigue.

But it happened to the lion's tail, as it did with the young men's chins, cheeks and upper lips. A beard did indeed grow, but once shaved off--and many did shave, thinking to promote greater growth--no more hair ever appeared again. The ointment forced a downy growth but it killed the roots of the hair.

A worse fate befell the lion. A crop of hair, perhaps an inch longer than common, grew out. But this time, the bad medicine, which had deceived men, and was unfit for lions, struck in.

From this cause, added to nervous prostration, old Leo fell dead. As lion fathers go, he was a good one, and his widow and children mourned for him. He had never once, however hungry, tried to eat up his cubs, which was something in his favor.

Soon after these exploits, the old artist died also. His son, hearing there was still a demand, among kings, for lions, and those especially with centre curls in their tails, took the most promising of the whelps and petted and fed him well. In the seventh year, when his mane and elbow and knee hair had grown out, this cub was mated to a young lioness of like promise. When, of this couple, a male whelp was born, it was found that in due time its knees, elbows, tail-tuft, and the front of its body were all rich in furry growth. In the middle of its tail, also, thick ringlets, several inches long, were growing. Evidently, the hair tonic had done some good. So this one became the father of all the curly-tailed lions in the Netherlands. Not only was this lion, thus distinguished for so novel an ornament, copied into heraldry, but it adorned many city seals and town arms. In time, the lion of the Netherlands was pictured with a crown on its head, a sword in its right hand, a bundle of seven arrows--in token of a union of seven states--and, still later, the new Order of the Netherlands Lion was founded. The original curly lion, with long hair in the middle of its tail, boasts of a long line of descendants that are proud of their ancestor.

BRABO AND THE GIANT

Ages ago, when the giants were numerous on the earth, there lived a big fellow named Antigonus. That was not what his mother had called him, but some one told him of a Greek general of that name; so he took this for his own. He was rough and cruel. His castle was on the Scheldt River, where the city of Antwerp now stands. Many ships sailed out of France and Holland, down this stream. They were loaded with timber, flax, iron, cheese, fish, bread, linen, and other things made in the country. It was by this trade that many merchants grew rich, and their children had plenty of toys to play with. The river was very grand, deep, and wide. The captains of the ships liked to sail on it, because there was no danger from rocks, and the country through which it flowed was so pretty.

So every day, one could see hundreds of white-sailed craft moving towards the sea, or coming in from the ocean. Boys and girls came down to stand in their wooden shoes on the banks, to see the vessels moving to and fro. The incoming ships brought sugar, wine, oranges, lemons, olives and other good things to eat, and wool to make warm clothes. Often craftsmen came from the wonderful countries in the south to tell of the rich cities there, and help to build new and fine houses, and splendid churches, and town halls. So all the Belgian people were happy.

But one day, this wicked giant came into the country to stop the ships and make them pay him money. He reared a strong castle on the river banks. It had four sides and high walls, and deep down in the earth were dark, damp dungeons. One had to light a candle to find his way to the horrid places.

What was it all for? The people wondered, but they soon found out. The giant, with a big knotted club, made out of an oak tree, strode through the town. He cried out to all the people to assemble in the great open square.

"From this day forth," he roared, "no ship, whether up or down the river, shall pass by this place, without my permission. Every captain must pay me toll, in money or goods. Whoever refuses, shall have both his hands cut off and thrown into the river.

"Hear ye all and obey. Any one caught in helping a ship go by without paying toll, whether it be night, or whether it be day, shall have his thumbs cut off and be put in the dark dungeon for a month. Again I say, Obey!"

With this, the giant swung and twirled his club aloft and then brought it down on a poor countryman's cart, smashing it into flinders. This was done to show his strength.

So every day, when the ships hove in sight, they were hailed from the giant's castle and made to pay heavy toll. Poor or rich, they had to hand over their money. If any captain refused, he was brought ashore and made to kneel before a block and place one hand upon the other. Then the giant swung his axe and cut off both hands, and flung them into the river. If a ship master hesitated, because he had no money, he was cast into a dungeon, until his friends paid his ransom.

Soon, on account of this, the city got a bad name. The captains from France kept in, and the ship men from Spain kept out. The merchants found their trade dwindling, and they grew poorer every day. So some of them slipped out of the city and tried to get the ships to sail in the night, and silently pass the giant's castle.

But the giant's watchers, on the towers, were as wide awake as owls and greedy as hawks. They pounced on the ship captains, chopped off their hands and tossed them into the river. The townspeople, who were found on board, were thrown into the dungeons and had their thumbs cut off.

So the prosperity of the city was destroyed, for the foreign merchants were afraid to send their ships into the giant's country. The reputation of the city grew worse. It was nicknamed by the Germans Hand Werpen, or Hand Throwing; while the Dutchmen called it Antwerp, which meant the same thing. The Duke of Brabant, or Lord of the land, came to the big fellow's fortress and told him to stop. He even shook his fist under the giant's huge nose, and threatened to attack his castle and burn it. But Antigonus only snapped his fingers, and laughed at him. He made his castle still stronger and kept on hailing ships, throwing some of the crews into dungeons and cutting off the hands of the captains, until the fish in the river grew fat.

Now there was a brave young fellow named Brabo, who lived in the province of Brabant. He was proud of his country and her flag of yellow, black and red, and was loyal to his lord. He studied the castle well and saw a window, where he could climb up into the giant's chamber.

Going to the Duke, Brabo promised if his lord's soldiers would storm the gates of the giant's castle, that he would seek out and fight the ruffian. While they battered down the gates, he would climb the walls. "He's nothing but a 'bulle-wak'" (a bully and a boaster), said Brabo, "and we ought to call him that, instead of Antigonus."

The Duke agreed. On a dark night, one thousand of his best men-at-arms were marched with their banners, but with no drums or trumpets, or anything that could make a noise and alarm the watchmen.

Reaching a wood full of big trees near the castle, they waited till after midnight. All the dogs in the town and country, for five miles around, were seized and put into barns, so as not to bark and wake the giant up. They were given plenty to eat, so that they quickly fell asleep and were perfectly quiet.

At the given signal, hundreds of men holding ship's masts, or tree trunks, marched against the gates. They punched and pounded and at last smashed the iron-bound timbers and rushed in. After overcoming the garrison, they lighted candles, and unlocking the dungeons, went down and set the poor half-starved captives free. Some of them pale, haggard and thin as hop poles, could hardly stand. About the same time, the barn doors where the dogs had been kept, were thrown open. In full cry, a regiment of the animals, from puppies to hounds, were at once out, barking, baying, and yelping, as if they knew what was going on and wanted to see the fun.

But where was the giant? None of the captains could find him. Not one of the prisoners or the garrison could tell where he had hid.

But Brabo knew that the big fellow, Antigonus, was not at all brave, but really only a bully and a coward. So the lad was not afraid. Some of his comrades outside helped him to set up a tall ladder against the wall. Then, while all the watchers and men-at-arms inside, had gone away to defend the gates, Brabo climbed into the castle, through a slit in the thick wall. This had been cut out, like a window, for the bow-and-arrow men, and was usually occupied by a sentinel. Sword in hand, Brabo made for the giant's own room. Glaring at the youth, the big fellow seized his club and brought it down with such force that it went through the wooden floor. But Brabo dodged the blow and, in a trice, made a sweep with his sword. Cutting off the giant's head, he threw it out the window. It had hardly touched the ground, before the dogs arrived. One of the largest of these ran away with the trophy and the big, hairy noddle of the bully was never found again.

But the giant's huge hands! Ah, they were cut off by Brabo, who stood on the very top of the highest tower, while all below looked up and cheered. Brabo laid one big hand on top of the other, as the giant used to do, when he cut off the hands of captains. He took first the right hand and then the left hand and threw them, one at a time, into the river.

A pretty sight now revealed the fact that the people knew what had been going on and were proud of Brabo's valor. In a moment, every house in Antwerp showed lighted candles, and the city was illuminated. Issuing from the gates came a company of maidens. They were dressed in white, but their leader was robed in yellow, red, and black, the colors of the Brabant flag. They all sang in chorus the praises of Brabo their hero.

"Let us now drop the term of disgrace to the city--that of the Hand-Throwing and give it a new name," said one of the leading men of Antwerp.

"No," said the chief ruler, "let us rather keep the name, and, more than ever, invite all peaceful ships to come again, 'an-'t-werf' (at the wharf), as of old. Then, let the arms of Antwerp be two red hands above a castle."

"Agreed," cried the citizens with a great shout. The Duke of Brabant approved and gave new privileges to the city, on account of Brabo's bravery. So, from high to low, all rejoiced to honor their hero, who was richly rewarded.

After this, thousands of ships, from many countries, loaded or unloaded their cargoes on the wharves, or sailed peacefully by. Antwerp excelled all seaports and became very rich again. Her people loved their native city so dearly, that they coined the proverb "All the world is a ring, and Antwerp is the pearl set in it."

To this day, in the great square, rises the splendid bronze monument of Brabo the Brave. The headless and handless hulk of the giant Antigonus lies sprawling, while on his body rests Antwerp castle. Standing over all, at the top, is Brabo high in air. He holds one of the hands of Antigonus, which he is about to toss into the Scheldt River.

No people honor valor more than the Belgians. Themselves are to-day, as of old, among the bravest.

THE FARM THAT RAN AWAY AND CAME BACK

There was once a Dutchman, who lived in the province called Drenthe. Because there was a row of little trees on his farm, his name was Ryer Van Boompjes; that is, Ryer of the Little Trees. After a while, he moved to the shore of the Zuyder Zee and into Overijssel. Overijssel means over the Ijssel River. There he bought a new farm, near the village of Blokzyl. By dyking and pumping, certain wise men had changed ten acres, of sand and heath, into pasture and land for plowing. They surrounded it on three sides with canals. The fourth side fronted on the Zuyder Zee. Then they advertised, in glowing language, the merits of the new land and Ryer Van Boompjes bought it and paid for his real estate. He was as proud as a popinjay of his island and he ruled over it like a Czar or a Kaiser.

A few years before, Ryer had married a "queezel," as the Dutch call either a nun, or a maid who is no longer young. At this date, when our story begins, he had four blooming, but old-fashioned children, with good appetites. They could eat cabbage and potatoes, rye bread and cheese, by the half peck, and drink buttermilk by the quart. In addition, Ryer owned four horses, six cows, two dogs, some roosters and hens, a flock of geese, two dozen ducks, and a donkey.

Yet although Ryer was rich, as wealth is reckoned in Drenthe, whence he had come, he was greedy for more. He skimped the food of his animals. So much did he do this, that his neighbors declared that they had seen him put green spectacles on his cows and the donkey. Then he mixed straws and shavings with the hay to make the animals think they were eating fresh grass.

When he ploughed, he drove his horses close to the edge next to the water, so as to make use of every half inch of land. When sometimes bits of fen land, from his neighbor's farms, got loose and floated on the water, Ryer felt he was in luck. He would go out at night, grapple the boggy stuff and fasten it to his own land.

After this had happened several times, and Ryer had added a half acre to his holdings, his greed possessed him like a bad fairy. He began to steal the land on the other side of the Zuyder Zee. In the course of time, he became a regular land thief. Whenever he saw, or heard of, a floating bit of territory, he rowed his boat after it by night. Before morning, aided by wicked helpers, who shared in the plunder, and were in his pay, he would have the bog attached to his own farm.

All this time, he hardly realized that his ill-gotten property, now increased to twelve acres or more, was itself a very shaky bit of real estate. In fact, it was not real at all. His wife one day told him so, for she knew of her mean husband's trickery.

About this time, heavy rains fell, for many days, and without ceasing, until all the region was reduced to pulp and the country seemed afloat. The dykes appeared ready to burst. Thousands feared that the land had an attack of the disease called val (fall) and that the soil would sink under the waves as portions of the realm had done before, in days long gone by.

Yet none of this impending trouble worried Ryer, whose greed grew by what it fed upon. In fact, the first day the sun shone again, quickly drying up parts of his farm, he had two horses harnessed up for work. Then he drove them so near the edge of the ditch that plough, man, and horses tumbled, and down they went, into the shiny mess of mud and water.

At this moment, also, the water, from below the bottom of the Zuyder Zee, welled up, in a great wave, like a mushroom, and the whole of Ryer's soggy estate was on the point of breaking loose and seemed ready to float away.

The stingy fellow, as he fell overboard, bumped his head so hard on the plough beam, that he lay senseless for a half hour. He would certainly have been drowned, had not Pete, his stout son, who was not far away, and had seen the tumble, ran to the house, launched a boat and rowed quickly to the spot, where he had last seen his father. Grabbing his daddy by the collar, he hauled him, half dead, into the boat. Between his bump and his fright, and the cold bath, old Ryer was a long time coming to his wits. With filial piety, Pete kept on rubbing the paternal hands and restoring the circulation. All this, however, took a long time, even an hour or more. When his father was able to sit up and talk, Pete started to row back to the little wharf in front of his home.

But where was it,--the farm, with the house and fields? Whither had they gone? Ryer was too mystified to get his bearings, but Pete knew the points of the compass. Yet his father's farm was not there. He looked at the shore of Overijssel, which he had left. Instead of the old, straight lines of willow trees, with the church spire beyond, there was a hollow and empty place. It looked as if a giant, as big as the world itself, had bitten out a piece of land and swallowed it down. Dumbfounded, father and son looked, the one at the other, but said nothing, for there was nothing to say.

Meanwhile, what had become of the farm and "the Queezel," as the neighbors still called her--that is, the mother with the children. These good people soon saw that they were floating off somewhere. The mainland was every moment receding further into the distance. In fact, the farm was moving from Overijssel northward, towards Friesland. One by one, the church spires of the village near by faded from sight.

But when the wind changed from south to west, they seemed as if on a ship, with sails set, and to be making due west, for North Holland. The younger children, so far from being afraid, clapped their hands in glee. They thought it great fun to ferry across the big water, which they had so long seen before their eyes. Their stingy father had never owned a carriage, or allowed the horses to be ridden. He always made his family walk to church. Whether it were to the sermon, in the morning, or to hear the catechism expounded by the Domine, in the afternoon, all the family had to tramp on their wooden shoes there and back.

As for the floating farm, the cows could not understand it. They mooed piteously, while the donkey brayed loudly. At night, and day after day, no one could attend properly to the animals, to see that they were fed and given water. One always sees a big tub in the middle of a Dutch pasture field. Neither ducks, nor geese, nor chickens minded it in the least, but the thirsty cattle and horses, at the end of the first day, had drunk the tub dry. None of the dumb brutes, even if they had not been afraid of being drowned, could drink from the Zuyder Zee, for it was chiefly sea water, that is, salt, or at least brackish.

Occasionally this errant farm, that had thus broken loose, passed by fishermen, who wondered at so much land thus adrift. Yet they feared to hail, and go on board, lest the owners might think them intruding. Others thought it none of their business, supposing some crazy fellow was using his farm as a ship, to move his lands, goods and household, and thus save expense. In some of the villages, the runaway farm was descried from the tops of the church towers. Then, it furnished a subject for chat and gossip, during three days, to the women, as they milked the cows, or knitted stockings. To the men, also, while they smoked, or drank their coffee, it was a lively topic.

"There were real people on it and a house and stables," said the sexton of a church, who declared that he had seen this new sort of a flying Dutchman. It was the usual sight--"cow, dog, and stork," and then he quoted the old Dutch proverb.

At last, after several days, and when Ryer and his son were nearly finished, with fatigue and fright, in trying to row their boat to catch up with the runaway farm, they finally reached a village across the Zuyder Zee, in North Holland, where rye bread and turnips satisfied their hunger and they had waffles for dessert. Their small change went quickly, and then the two men were at their wit's end to know what further to do.

By this time, out on the floating farm, the mother and children were wild with fear of starving. All the food for the cattle had been eaten up, the dog had no meat, the cat no milk, and the stork had run out of its supply of frogs. There was no sugar or coffee, and neither rye nor currant-bread, or sliced sausage or wafer-thin cheese for any one; but only potatoes and some barley grain. Happily, however, in drifting within sight of the village of Osterbeek, the mother and the children noticed that the east wind was freshening. Soon they descried the tops of the church towers of North Holland. The smell of cows and cheese and of burning peat fires from the chimneys made both animals and human beings happy, as the wind blew the island westward to the village.

Curiously enough, this was the very place at which, by hard rowing, Ryer and Pete had also arrived. Father and son were sitting in the hotel parlor, with their eyes down on the sandy floor, wondering how they were to pay for their next sandwich and coffee, for their money was all gone.

At that moment, a small boy clattered over the bricks in his klomps. He kicked these off, at the door, and rushed into the room. He had on his yellow baggy trousers and his hair, of the same color, was cut level with his ears. Half out of breath, he announced the coming, afloat, of what looked like a combination of farm and menagerie. A house, a woman, some girls, a dog, a cat, and a stork were on it and afloat.

At once, old man Ryer, still stiff from his long, cold bath, hobbled out, and Pete ran before him. Yes, it was mother, the children and all the animals! For the first time in his life, the mean old sinner felt his heart thumping, in grateful emotion, under his woolen jacket, with its two gold buttons. Something like real religion had finally oozed out from under his crusted soul.

A whole convoy of boys, fishermen, farmers, and a fat vrouw or two, volunteered to go out and tow the runaway farm to the village wharf. They succeeded in grappling the float and held it fast by ropes tied to a horse post.

That night all were happy. The farm was made fast by another rope put round the town pump. Then the villagers all went to bed. They were happy in having rescued a runaway farm, and they expected a good "loon" (reward) from the rich old Ryer, who, in the barroom, had talked big about his wealth.

As for the Van Boompjes, in order to save a landlord's bill for beds, they slept in their house, on board the farm, amid the lowing of their cattle that called out, in their own way, for more fodder; while the people in the village wondered at roosters crowing out on the water, and evidently the barn-yard birds were frightened.

And so they were; for, before midnight, when all other creatures were asleep, and not even a mouse was stirring on land, whether hard fast, or floating, the west wind rose mightily and blew to a terrific gale.

In a moment, the tow lines, that held the vagrant farm to the village pump and horse post, snapped. The Van Boompjes estate left the wharf and was driven, at a furious rate, across the Zuyder Zee. For several hours, like a ship under full sail, it was pushed westward by the wind. Yet so soundly did all sleep, man and wife, children and hens, that none awakened during this strange voyage. Even the roosters, after their first concert, held in their voices.

Suddenly, and as straight as if steered by a skilled pilot, the Van Boompjes farm, now an accomplished traveller, after its many adventures, shot into its old place. This took place with such violence, that Ryer Van Boompjes and his wife were both thrown out of bed. The cows were knocked over in the stable. The dog barked, supposing some one had kicked him. One old rooster, jostled off his perch, set up a tremendous crowing, that brought some of the early risers out to rub their eyes and see what was going on.

"Hemel en aard, bliksem en regen" (Heaven and earth, lightning and rain), they cried, "the old farm is back in its place."

In fact, the Van Boompjes real estate was snugly fitted once more to the mainland, and again in the niche it had left. It had struck so hard, that a ridge of raised sod, five inches high, marked the place of junction. At least twenty fishes and wriggling eels were smashed in the collision.

From that day forth the conscience of Van Boompjes returned, and he actually became an honest man. He sawed off, from time to time, portions of his big farm, and returned them home, with money paid as interest, to the owners. He found out all the mynheers, whose bits of land had drifted off. He sent a tidy sum of gold to the village in North Holland, where his farm had been moored, for a few hours. With a good conscience, he went to church and worshipped. His action, at each of the two collections, which Dutch folks always take up on Sundays, was noticed and praised as a sure and public sign of the old sinner's true repentance. When the deacons, with their white gloves on, poked under his nose their black velvet bags, hung at the end of fishing poles, ten feet long, this man, who had been for years a skinflint, dropped in a silver coin each time.

On the farm, all the animals, from duck to stork, and from dog to ox, now led happier lives. In the family, all declared that the behavior of the farm and the wind of the Zuyder Zee had combined to make a new man and a delightful father of old Van Boompjes. He lived long and happily and died greatly lamented.

SANTA KLAAS AND BLACK PETE

Who is Santa Klaas? How did he get his name? Where does he live? Did you ever see him?

These are questions, often asked of the storyteller, by little folks.

Before Santa Klaas came into the Netherlands, that is, to Belgium and Holland, he was called by many names, in the different countries in which he lived, and where he visited. Some people say he was born in Myra, many hundred years ago before the Dutch had a dyke or a windmill, or waffles, or wooden shoes. Others tell us how, in time of famine, the good saint found the bodies of three little boys, pickled in a tub, at a market for sale, and to be eaten up. They had been salted down to keep till sold. The kind gentleman and saint, whose name was Nicholas, restored these three children to life. It is said that once he lost his temper, and struck with his fist a gentleman named Arius; but the story-teller does not believe this, for he thinks it is a fib, made up long afterward. How could a saint lose his temper so?

Another story they tell of this same Nicholas was this. There were three lovely maidens, whose father had lost all his money. They wanted husbands very badly, but had no money to buy fine clothes to get married in. He took pity on both their future husbands and themselves. So he came to the window, and left three bags of gold, one after the other. Thus these three real girls all got real husbands, just as the novels tell us of the imaginary ones. They lived happily ever afterward, and never scolded their husbands.

By and by, men who were goldsmiths, bankers or pawnbrokers, made a sign of these three bags of gold, in the shape of balls. Now they hang them over their shop doors, two above one. This means "two to one, you will never get it again"--when you put your ring, furs, or clothes, or watch, or spoons, in pawn.

It is ridiculous how many stories they do tell of this good man, Nicholas, who was said to be what they call a bishop, or inspector, who goes around seeing that things are done properly in the churches. It was because the Reverend Mr. Nicholas had to travel about a good deal, that the sailors and travellers built temples and churches in his honor. To travel, one must have a ship on the sea and a horse on the land, or a reindeer up in the cold north;

though now, it is said, he comes to Holland in a steamship, and uses an automobile.

On Santa Klaas eve, each of the Dutch children sets out in the chimney his wooden shoe. Into it, he puts a whisp of hay, to feed the traveller's horse. When St. Nicholas first came to Holland, he arrived in a sailing ship from Spain and rode on a horse. Now he arrives in a big steamer, made of steel. Perhaps he will come in the future by aeroplane. To fill all the shoes and stockings, the good saint must have an animal to ride. Now the fast white horse, named Sleipnir, was ready for him, and on Sleipnir's back he made his journeys.

How was Santa Klaas dressed?

His clothes were those of a bishop. He wore a red coat and his cap, higher than a turban and called a mitre, was split along two sides and pointed at the top. In his hands, he held a crozier, which was a staff borrowed from shepherds, who tended sheep; and with the crozier he helped the lambs over rough places; but the crozier of Santa Klaas was tipped with gold. He had white hair and rosy cheeks. For an old man, he was very active, but his heart and feelings never got to be one day older than a boy's, for these began when mother love was born and father's care was first in the world, but it never grows old.

When Santa Klaas travelled up north to Norway and into the icy cold regions, where there were sleighs and reindeer, he changed his clothes. Instead of his red robe, he wears a jacket, much shorter and trimmed with ermine, white as snow. Taking off his mitre, he wears a cap of fur also, and has laid aside his crozier. In the snow, wheels are no good, and runners are the best for swift travel. So, instead of his white horse and a wagon, he drives in a sleigh, drawn by two stags with large horns. In every country, he puts into the children's stockings hung up, or shoes set in the fireplace, something which they like. In Greenland, for example, he gives the little folks seal blubber, and fish hooks. So his presents are not the same in every country. However, for naughty boys and girls everywhere, instead of filling shoes and stockings, he may leave a switch, or pass them by empty.

When Santa Klaas travels, he always brings back good things. Now when he first came to New Netherland in America, what did he find to take back to Holland?

Well, it was here, on our continent, that he found corn, potatoes, pumpkins, maple sugar, and something to put in pipes to smoke; besides strange birds and animals, such as turkeys and raccoons, in addition to many new flowers. What may be called a weed, like the mullein, for example, is considered very pretty in Europe, where they did not have such things. There it is called the American Velvet Plant, or the King's Candlestick.

But, better than all, Santa Klaas found a negro boy, Pete, who became one of the most faithful of his helpers. At Utrecht, in Holland, the students of the University give, every year, a pageant representing Santa Klaas on his white horse, with Black Pete, who is always on hand and very busy. Black Pete's father brought peanuts from Africa to America, and sometimes Santa Klaas drops a bagful of these, as a great curiosity, into the shoes of the Dutch young folks.

Santa Klaas was kept very busy visiting the homes and the public schools in New Netherland; for in these schools all the children, girls as well as boys, and not boys only, received a free education. In later visits he heard of Captain Kidd and his fellow pirates, who wore striped shirts and red caps, and had pigtails of hair, tied in eel skins, and hanging down their backs. These fellows wore earrings and stuck pistols in their belts and daggers at their sides. Instead of getting their gold honestly, and giving it to the poor, or making presents to the children, the pirates robbed ships. Then, as 'twas said, they buried their treasure. Lunatics and boys that read too many novels, have ever since been digging in the land to find Captain Kidd's gold.

Santa Klaas does not like such people. Moreover, he was just as good to the poor slaves, as to white children. So the colored people loved the good saint also. Their pickaninnies always hung up their stockings on the evening of December sixth.

Santa Klaas filled the souls of the people in New Netherland so full of his own spirit, that now children all over the United States, and those of Americans living in other countries, hang up their stockings and look for a visit from him.

In Holland, Black Pete was very loyal and true to his master, carrying not only the boxes and bundles of presents for the good children, but also the switches for bad boys and girls. Between the piles of pretty things to surprise good children, on one side, and the boxes of birch and rattan, the straps and hard hair-brush backs for naughty youngsters, Pete holds the horn of plenty. In this are dolls, boats, trumpets, drums, balls, toy houses, flags, the animals in Noah's Ark, building blocks, toy castles and battleships, story and picture books, little locomotives, cars, trains, automobiles, aeroplanes, rocking horses, windmills, besides cookies, candies, marbles, tops, fans, lace, and more nice things than one can count.

Pete also takes care of the horse of Santa Klaas, named Sleipnir, which goes so fast that, in our day, the torpedo and submarine U-boats are named after him. This wonderful animal used to have eight feet, for swiftness. That was when Woden rode him, but, in course of time, four of his legs dropped off, so that the horse of Santa Klaas looks less like a centipede and more like other horses. Whenever Santa Klaas walks, Pete has to go on foot also, even though the chests full of presents for the children are very heavy and Pete has to carry them.

Santa Klaas cares nothing about rich girls or poor girls, for all the kinds of boys he knows about or thinks of are good boys and bad boys. A youngster caught stealing jam out of the closet, or cookies from the kitchen, or girls lifting lumps of sugar out of the sugar bowl, or eating too much fudge, or that are mean, stingy, selfish, or have bad tempers, are considered naughty and more worthy of the switch than of presents. So are the boys who attend Sunday School for a few weeks before Christmas, and then do not come any more till next December. These Santa Klaas turns over to Pete, to be well thrashed.

In Holland, Pete still keeps on the old dress of the time of New Netherland. He wears a short jacket, with wide striped trousers, in several bright colors, shoes strapped on his feet, a red cap and a ruff around his neck. Sometimes he catches bad boys, to put them in a bag for a half hour, to scare them; or, he shuts them up in a dark closet, or sends them to bed without any supper. Or, instead of allowing them eleven buckwheat cakes at breakfast, he makes them stop at five. When Santa Klaas leaves Holland to go back to Spain, or elsewhere, Pete takes care of the nag Sleipnir, and hides himself until Santa Klaas comes again next year.

The story-teller knows where Santa Klaas lives, but he won't tell.

THE GOBLINS TURNED TO STONE

When the cow came to Holland, the Dutch folks had more and better things to eat. Fields of wheat and rye took the place of forests. Instead of acorns and the meat of wild game, they now enjoyed milk and bread. The youngsters made pets of the calves and all the family lived under one roof. The cows had a happy time of it, because they were kept so clean, fed well, milked regularly, and cared for in winter.

By and by the Dutch learned to make cheese and began to eat it every day. They liked it, whether it was raw, cooked, toasted, sliced, or in chunks, or served with other good things. Even the foxes and wild creatures were very fond of the smell and taste of toasted cheese. They came at night close to the houses, often stealing the cheese out of the pantry. When a fox would not, or could not, be caught in a trap by any other bait, a bit of cooked cheese would allure him so that he was caught and his fur made use of.

When the people could not get meat, or fish, they had toasted bread and cheese, which in Dutch is "geroostered brod met kaas." Then they laughed, and named the new dish after whatever they pretended it was. It was just the same, as when they called goodies, made out of flour and sugar, "nuts," "fingers," "calves" and "lambs." Even grown folks love to play and pretend things like children.

Soon, it became the fashion to have cheese parties. Men and women would sit around the fire, by the hour, nibbling the toast that had melted cheese poured over it. But after they had gone to bed, some of them dreamed.

Now some dreams may be pleasant, but cheese-dreams were not usually of this sort. The dreamer thought that a big she-horse had climbed upon the bed and sat down upon his stomach. Once there, the beast grinned hideously, snored, and pressed its hoofs down on the sleeper's breast, so that he could not breathe or speak. The feeling was a horrible one; but, just when the dreamer expected to choke, he seemed to jump off some high place, and come down somewhere, very far off. Then the animal ran away and the terrible dream was over.

This was called a nightmare, or in Dutch a "nacht merrie." "Nacht" means night, and "merrie" a filly or a mare. In the dream, it was not a small or a young horse, but always a big mare that squatted down on a man's stomach.

In those days, instead of seeking for the trouble inside, or asking whether there was any connection between nightmares and too hearty eating of cheese, the Dutch fathers laid it all on the goblins.

The goblins, or sooty elves, that used to live in Holland, were ugly, short fellows, very smart, quick in action and able to travel far in a second. They were first cousins to the kabouters. They had big heads, green eyes and split feet, like cows. They were so ugly, that they were ordered to live under ground and never come out during the day. If they did, they would be turned to stone.

The goblins had a bad reputation for mischief. They liked to have fun with human beings. They would listen to the conversation of people and then mock them by repeating the last word. That is the reason why echoes were called "week klank," or dwarf's talk.

Because these goblins were short, they envied men their greater stature and wanted to grow to the height of human beings. As they were not able of themselves to do this, they often sneaked into a house and snatched a child out of the cradle. In place of the stolen baby, one of their own wizened children was laid. That was the reason why many a poor little baby, that grew puny and thin, was called a "wiseel-kind," or changeling. When the sick baby could not get well, and medicine or care seemed to do no good, the mother thought that the goblins had taken away her own child.

It was only the female goblins that would change themselves into night mares and sit on the body of the dreamer. They usually came in through a hole or a crack; but if that person in the house could plug up the hole, or stop the crack, he could conquer the female goblin, and do what he pleased with her. If a man wanted to, he could make her his wife. So long as the hole was kept stopped up, by which the goblin entered, she made a good wife. If this crack was left open, or if the plug dropped out of the hole, the she-goblin was off and could never be found again.

The ruler of the goblins lived beneath the earth, as the king of the underworld. His palace was made of gold and glittered with gems. He had riches more than men could count. All the goblins and kabouters, who worked in the mines and at the forges and anvils, making swords, spears, bells, or jewels, obeyed him.

The most wonderful things about these dwarfs was the way in which they made themselves invisible, so that men were able to see neither the night mares nor the male goblins, while at their mischief. This was a little red cap which every goblin possessed, and which he was careful never to lose. The red cap acted like a snuffer on a candle, to put it out, and while under it, no goblin could be seen by mortal eyes.

Now it happened that one night, as a dear old lady lay dying on her bed, a middle-sized goblin, with his red cap on, came in through a crack into the room, and stood at the foot of her bed. Just for mischief and to frighten her by making himself visible, he took off his red cap.

When the old lady saw the imp, she cried out loudly:

"Go way, go way. Don't you know I belong to my Lord?"

But the goblin dwarf only laughed at her, with his green eyes.

Calling her daughter Alida, the old lady whispered in her ear:

"Bring me my wooden shoes."

Rising up in her bed, the old lady hurled the heavy klomps, one after the other, at the goblin's head. At this, he started to get out through the crack, and away, but before his body was half out, Alida snatched his red cap away. Then she stuck a needle in his cloven foot that made him howl with pain. Alida looked at the crack through which he escaped and found it quite sooty.

Twirling the little red cap around on her forefinger, a brilliant thought struck her. She went and told the men her plan, and they agreed to it. This was to gather hundreds of farmers and townfolk, boys and men together, on the next moonlight night, and round up all the goblins in Drenthe. By pulling off their caps, and holding them till the sun rose, when they would be petrified, the whole brood could be exterminated.

So, knowing that the goblin would come the next night, to steal back his red cap, she left a note outside the crack, telling him to bring several hundred goblins to the great moor, or veldt. There, at a certain hour near midnight, he would find the red cap on a bush. With his companions, he could celebrate the return of the cap. In exchange for this, she asked the goblin to bring her a gold necklace.

The moonlight night came round and hundreds of the men of Drenthe gathered together. They were armed with horseshoes, and with witch-hazel and other plants, which are like poison to the sooty elves. They had also bits of parchment covered with runes, a strange kind of writing, and various charms which are supposed to be harmful to goblins. It was agreed to move together in a circle towards the centre, where the lady Alida was to hang the red cap upon a bush. Then, with a rush, the men were to snatch off all the goblins' caps, pulling and grabbing, whether they could see, or even feel anything, or not.

The placing of the red cap upon the bush in the centre, by the lady Alida, was the signal.

So, when the great round-up narrowed to a small space, the men began to grab, snatch and pull. Putting their hands out in the air, at the height of about a yard from the ground, they hustled and pushed hard. In a few minutes, hundreds of red caps were in their hands, and as many goblins became visible. They were, indeed, an ugly host.

Yet hundreds of other goblins escaped, with their caps on, and were still invisible. As they broke away in groups, however, they were seen, for in each bunch was one or more visible fellow, because he was capless. So the men divided into squads, to chase the imps a long distance, even to many distant places. It was a most curious night battle. Here could be seen groups of men in a tussle with the goblins, many more of which, but by no means all, were made capless and visible.

The racket kept up till the sky in the east was gray. Had all the goblins run away, it would have been well with them. Hundreds of them did, but the others were so anxious to help their fellows, or to get back their own caps, fearing the disgrace of returning head bare to their king, and getting a good scolding, that the sun suddenly rose on them, before they knew it was day.

At the first level ray, the goblins were all turned to stone.

The treeless, desolate land, which, a moment before, was full of struggling goblins and men, became as quiet as the blue sky above. Nothing but some rounded rocks or stones, in groups, marked the spot where the bloodless battle of imps and men had been fought.

There, these stones, big and little, lie to this day. Among the buckwheat, and the potato blossoms of the summer, under the shadows and clouds, and whispering breezes of autumn, or covered with the snows of winter, they are seen on desolate heaths. Over some of them, oak trees, centuries old, have grown. Others are near, or among, the farmers' grain fields, or, not far from houses and barn-yards. The cows wander among them, knowing nothing of their past. And the goblins come no more.

THE MOULDY PENNY

"Gold makes a woman penny-white," said the Dutch, in the days when fairies were plentiful and often in their thoughts. What did the proverb mean? Who ever saw a white penny?

Well, that was long ago, when pennies were white, because they were then made of silver. Each one was worth a denary, which was a coin worth about a shilling, or a quarter of a dollar.

As the Dutch had pounds, shillings and pence, before the English had them, we see what *d* in the signs £ s. d. means, that is, a denary, or a white penny, made of silver.

In the old days, before the Dutch had houses with glass windows or clothes of cloth or linen, or hats or shoes, cows and horses, or butter and cheese, they knew nothing of money and they cared less. Almost everything, even the land, was owned in common by all. Their wants were few. Whenever they needed anything from other countries they swapped or bartered. In this way they traded salt for furs, or fish for iron. But when they met with, or had to fight, another tribe that was stronger or richer, or knew more than they did, they required other things, which the forests and waters could not furnish. So, by and by, pedlars and merchants came up from the south. They brought new and strange articles, such as mirrors, jewelry, clothes, and pretty things, which the girls and women wanted and had begged their daddies and husbands to get for them. For the men, they brought iron tools and better weapons, improved traps, to catch wild beasts, and wagons, with wheels that had spokes. When regular trade began, it became necessary to have money of some kind.

Then coins of gold, silver, and copper were seen in the towns and villages, and even in the woods and on the heaths of Holland. Yet there was a good deal that was strange and mysterious about these round, shining bits of metal, called money.

"Money. What is money?" asked many a proud warrior disdainfully.

Then the wise men explained to the fighting men, that money was named after Juno Moneta, a goddess in Rome. She told men that no one would ever want for money who was honest and just. Then, by and by, the mint was in her temple and money was coined there. Then, later, in Holland, the word meant money, but many people, who wanted to get rich quickly, worshipped her. In time, however, the word "gold" meant money in general.

When a great ruler, named Charlemagne, conquered or made treaties with our ancestors, he allowed them to have mints and to coin money. Then, again, it seemed wonderful how the pedlars and the goldsmiths and the men called Lombards--strange long-bearded men from the south, who came among the Dutch--grew rich faster than the work people. They seemed to amass gold simply by handling money.

When a man who knew what a silver penny would do, made a present of one to his wife, her face lighted up with joy. So in time, the word "penny white," meant the smiling face of a happy woman. Yet it was also noticed that the more people had, the more they wanted. The girls and boys quickly found that money would buy what the pedlars brought. In the towns, shops sprang up, in which were many curious things, which tempted people to buy.

Some tried to spend their money and keep it too--to eat their cake and have it also--but they soon found that they could not do this. There were still many foolish, as well as wise people, in the land, even during the new time of money. A few saved their coins and were happy in giving some to the poor and needy. Many fathers had what was called a "sparpot," or home savings bank, and taught their children the right use of money. It began to be the custom for people to have family names, so that a girl was not merely the daughter of so-and-so, nor a boy the son of a certain father. In the selection of names, those which had the word "penny" in them proved to be very popular. To keep a coin in the little home bank, without spending it, long enough for it to gather mould, which it did easily in the damp climate of Holland, that is, to darken and get a crust on it, was considered a great virtue in the owner. This showed that the owner had a strong mind and power of self-control. So the name "Schimmelpennig," or "mouldy penny," became honorable, because such people were wise and often kind and good. They did not waste their money, but made good use of it.

On the other hand, were some mean and stingy folks, who liked to hear the coins jingle. Instead of wisely spending their cash, or trading with it, they hoarded their coins; that is, they hid them away in a stocking, or a purse, or in a jar, or a cracked cooking pot, that couldn't be used. Often they put it away somewhere in the chimney, behind a loose brick. Then, at night, when no one was looking, these miserly folks counted, rubbed, jingled, and gloated over the shining coins and never helped anybody. So there grew up three sorts of people, called the thrifty, the spendthrifts, and the misers. These last were the meanest and most disliked of all. Others, again, hid their money away, so as to have some, when sick, or old, and they talked about it. No one found fault with these, though some laughed and said "a penny in the savings jar makes more noise than when it is full of gold." Even when folks got married they were exhorted by the minister to save money, "so as to have something to give to the poor."

Now when the fairies, that work down underground, heard that the Dutch had learned the use of money, and had even built a mint to stamp the metal, they held a feast to talk over what they should do to help or harm. In any event, they wanted to have some fun with the mortals above ground.

That has always been the way with kabouters. They are in for fun, first, last, and always. So, with punches and hammers, they made counterfeit money. Then, in league with the elves, they began also to delude misers and make them believe that much money makes men happy.

A long time after the mint had been built, two kabouters met to talk over their adventures.

"It is wonderful what fools these creatures called men are," said the first one. "There's old Vrek. He has been hoarding coins for the last fifty years. Now, he has a pile of gold in guilders and stivers, but there's hardly anything of his old self left. His soul is as small as a shrimp. I whispered to him not to let out his money in trade, but to keep it shut up. His strong box is full to bursting, but what went into the chest has oozed out of the man. He died, last night, and hardly anybody considers him worth burying. Some one on the street to-day asked what Vrek had left behind. The answer was 'Nothing--he took it all with him, for he had so little to take.'"

"That's jolly," said the older kabouter, who was a wicked looking fellow. "I'll get some fun out of this. To shrivel up souls will be my business henceforth. There's nothing like this newfangled business of getting money, that will do it so surely."

So this ugly old imp went "snooping" around, as the Dutch say, about people who sneak and dodge in and out of places, to which they ought not to go, and in houses where they should not be found. This imp's purpose was to make men crazy on the subject of making money, when they tried, as many of them did, to get rich quickly in mean ways. Sorry to tell, the imp found a good many promising specimens to work upon, at his business of making some wise men foolish. He taught them to take out of their souls what they hoarded away. To such fellows, when they became misers, he gave the name of "Schim," which means a shadow. It was believed by some people that such shrivelled up wretches had no bowels.

Soon after this, a great meeting of kabouters was held, in the dark realms below ground. Each one told what he had been doing on the earth. After the little imps had reported, the chief kabouter, when his turn came, cried out:

"I shall tell of three brothers, and what each one did with the first silver penny he earned."

"Go on," they all cried.

"I've caught one schim young. He married a wife only last year, but he won't give her one gulden a year to dress on. He skimps the table, pares the cheese till the rind is as thin as paper, and makes her live on skim milk and barley. Besides this, he won't help the poor with a stiver. I saw him put away a bright and shining silver penny, fresh from the mint. He hid coin and pocketbook in the bricks of a chimney. So I climbed down from the roof, seized both and ran away. I smeared the purse with wax and hid it in the thick rib of a boat, by the wharf. There the penny will gather mould enough. Ha! Ha! Ha!"

At this, the little imps broke out into a titter that sounded like the cackle of a hen trying to tell she had laid an egg.

"Good for you! Serves the old schim right," said a good kabouter, who loved to help human beings. "Now, I'll tell you about his brother, who has a wife and baby. He feeds and clothes them well, and takes good care of his old mother.

"Almost every week he helps some poor little boy, or girl, that has no mother or father. I heard him say he wished he could take care of poor orphans. So, when he was asleep, at night, I whispered in his ear and made him dream.

"'Put away your coin where it won't get mouldy and show that a penny that keeps moving is not like a rolling stone that gathers no moss. Deliver it to the goldsmiths for interest and leave it in your will to increase, until it becomes a great sum. Then, long after you are dead, the money you have saved and left for the poor *weesies* (orphans) will build a house for them. It will furnish food and beds and pay for nurses that will care for them, and good women who will be like mothers. Other folks, seeing what you have done, will build orphan houses. Then we shall have a Wees House (orphan asylum) in every town. No child, without a father or mother, in all Holland, will have to cry for milk or bread. Don't let your penny mould.'

"The third brother, named Spill-penny, woke up on the same morning, with a headache. He remembered that he had spent his silver penny at the gin house, buying drinks for a lot of worthless fellows like himself. He and his wife, with little to eat, had to wear ragged clothes, and the baby had not one toy to play with. When his wife gently chided him, he ran out of the house in bad humor. Going to the tap room, he ordered a drink of what we call 'Dutch courage,' that is, a glass of gin, and drank it down. Then what do you think he did?"

"Tell us," cried the imps uproariously.

"He went into a clothing house, bought a suit of clothes, and had it 'charged.'"

"That's it. I've known others like him," said an old imp.

"Now it was kermiss day in the village, and all that afternoon and evening this spendthrift was roystering with his fellow 'zuip zaks' (boon companions). With them, it was 'always drunk, always dry.' Near midnight, being too full of gin, he stumbled in the gutter, struck his head on the curb, and fell down senseless.

"Her husband not coming home that night, the distracted wife went out early in the morning. She found several men lying asleep on the sidewalks or in the gutters. She turned each one over, just as she did buckwheat cakes on the griddle, to see if this man or that was hers. At last she discovered her worthless husband, but no shaking or pulling could awake him. He was dead.

"Now there was a covetous undertaker in town, who carted away the corpse, and then told the widow that she must spend much money on the funeral, in order to have her husband buried properly; or else, the tongues of the neighbors would wag. So the poor woman had to sell her cow, the only thing she had, and was left poorer than ever. That was the end of Spill-penny."

"A jolly story," cried the kabouters in chorus. "Served him right. Now tell us about Vrek the miser. Go on."

"Well, the saying 'Much coin, much care,' is hardly true of him, for I and my trusty helpers ran away with all he had. With his first silver penny he began to hoard his money. He has been hunting for years for that penny, but has not found it. It will be rather mouldy, should he find it, but that he never will."

"Why not?" asked a young imp.

"For a good reason. He would not pay his boatmen their wages. So they struck, and refused to work. When he tried to sail his own boat, it toppled over and sunk, and Vrek was drowned. His wife was saved the expenses of a funeral, for his carcass was never found, and the covetous undertaker lost a job."

"What of the third one?" they asked.

"Oh, Mynheer Eerlyk, you mean? No harm can come to him. Everybody loves him and he cares for the orphans. There will be no mouldy penny in his house."

Then the meeting broke up. The good kabouters were happy. The bad ones, the imps, were sorry to miss what they hoped would be a jolly story.

When a thousand years passed away and the age of newspapers and copper pennies had come, there were no descendants of the two brothers Spill-penny and Schim; but of Mynheer Eerlyk there were as many as the years that had flown since he made a will. In this document, he ordered that his money, in guilders of gold and pennies of silver, should remain at compound interest for four hundred years. In time, the ever increasing sum passed from the goldsmiths to the bankers, and kept on growing enormously. At last this large fortune was spent in building hundreds of homes for orphans.

According to his wish, each girl in the asylum dressed in clothes that were of the colors on the city arms. In Amsterdam, for example, each orphan child's frock is half red and half black, with white aprons, and the linen and lace caps are very neat and becoming to their rosy faces. In Friesland, where golden hair and apple blossom cheeks are so often seen with the white lace and linen, some one has called the orphan girls "Apples of gold in pictures of silver." Among the many glories of the Netherlands is her care for the aged and the orphans.

One of the thirty generations of the Eerlyks read one day in the newspaper:

"Last week, while digging a very deep canal, some workman struck his pickaxe against timbers that were black with age, and nearly as hard as stone. These, on being brought up, showed that they were the ribs of an ancient boat. Learned men say that there was once a river here, which long since dried up. All the pieces of the boat were recovered, and, under the skilful hands of our ship carpenters, have been put together and the whole vessel is now set up and on view in our museum."

"We'll go down to-morrow on our way home from school, and see the curiosity," cried one of the Eerlyk boys, clapping his hands.

"Wait," said his father, "there's more in the story.

"To-day, the janitor of the museum, while examining a wide crack in one of the ribs, which was covered with wax, picked this substance away. He poked his finger in the crack, and finding something soft, pulled it out.

It was a rough leather purse, inside of which was a coin, mouldy with age and dark as the wood. Even after cleaning it with acid, it was hard to read what was stamped on it; but, strange to say, the face of the coin had left its impression on the leather, which had been covered with wax. From this, though the metal of the coin was black, and the mould thick on the coin, what they saw showed that it was a silver penny of the age of Charlemagne, or the ninth century."

"Charlemagne is French, father, but we call him Karel de Groot, or Charles the Great."

"Yes, my son. Don't you hear Karel's Klok (the curfew) sounding? 'Tis time for little folks to go to bed."

THE GOLDEN HELMET

For centuries, more than can be counted on the fingers of both hands, the maidens and mothers of Friesland have worn a helmet of gold covering the crown and back of their heads, and with golden rosettes at each ear. It marks the Frisian girl or woman. She is thus known by this head-dress as belonging to a glorious country, that has never been conquered and is proudly called Free Frisia. It is a relic of the age of gold, when this precious metal was used in a thousand forms, not seen to-day.

Of how and why the golden helmet is worn, this is the story:

In days gone by, when forests covered the land and bears and wolves were plentiful, there were no churches in Friesland. The people were pagans and all worshipped Woden, whom the Frisians called Fos-i-te'. Certain trees were sacred to him. When a baby was ill, or grown people had a disease, which medicine could not help, they laid the sick one at the foot of the holy tree, hoping for health soon to come. But, should the patient die under the tree, then the sorrowful friends were made glad, if the leaves of the tree fell upon the corpse. It was death to any person who touched the sacred tree with an axe, or made kindling wood, even of its branches.

Now among the wild people of the north, who ate acorns and were clothed in the skins of animals, there came, from the Christian lands of the south, a singer with his harp. Invited to the royal court, he sang sweet songs. To these the king's daughter listened with delight, until the tears, first of sorrow and then of joy, rolled down her lovely cheeks.

This maiden was the pride of her father, because of her sweet temper and willing spirit, while all the people boasted of her beauty. Her eyes were of the color of a sky without clouds. No spring flower could equal the pink and rose in her cheeks. Her lips were like the red coral, which the ship men brought from distant shores. Her long tresses rivalled gold in their glory. And, because her father worshipped Fos-i-té', the god of justice, and his daughter was always so fair to all her playmates, he, in his pride of her, gave her the name Fos-te-dí'-na, that is, the darling of Fos-i-té', or the Lady of Justice.

The singer from the south sang a new song, and when he played upon his harp his music was apt to be soft and low; sometimes sad, even, and often appealing. It was so much finer, and oh! so different, from what the glee men and harpers in the king's court usually rendered for the listening warriors. Instead of being about fighting and battle, or the hunting of wolves and bears, of stags and the aurochs, it was of healing the sick and helping the weak. In place of battles and the exploits of war lords, in fighting and killing Danes, the harper's whole story was of other things and about gentle people. He sang neither of war, nor of the chase, nor of fighting gods, nor of the storm maidens, that carry up to the sky, and into the hall of Woden, the souls of the slain on the battlefield. The singer sang of the loving Father in Heaven, who sent his dear Son to earth to live and die, that men might be saved. He made music with voice and instrument about love, and hope, and kindness to the sick and poor, of charity to widows and to orphans, and about the delights of doing good. He closed by telling the story of the crown of thorns, how wicked men nailed this good prophet to a cross, and how, when tender-hearted women wept, the Holy Teacher told them not to weep for him, but for themselves and their children. This mighty lord of noble thoughts and words lived what he taught. He showed greatness in the hour of death, by first remembering his mother, and then by forgiving his enemies.

"What! forgive an enemy? Forgive even the Danes? What horrible doctrine do we hear!" cried the men of war. "Let us kill this singer from the south." And they beat their swords on their metal shields, till the clangor was deafening. The great hall rang with echoes of the din, as if for battle. The Druids, or pagan priests, even more angry, applauded the action of the fighting men.

But Fos-te-dí-na rushed forward to shield the harper, and her long golden hair covered him.

"No!" said the king to his warriors. "This man is my guest. I invited him and he shall be safe here."

Sullen and bitter in their hearts, both priests and war men left the hall, breathing out revenge and feeling bound to kill the singer. Soon all were quiet in slumber, for the hour was late.

Why were the pagan followers of the king so angry with the singer?

The answer to this question is a story in itself.

Only three days before, a party of Christian Danes had been taken prisoners in the forest. They had come, peaceably and without arms, into the country; for they wanted to tell the Frisians about the new religion, which they had themselves received. In the cold night air, they had, unwittingly, cut off some of the dead branches of a tree sacred to the god Fos-i-té to kindle a fire.

A spy, who had closely watched them, ran and told his chief. Now, the Christian Danes were prisoners and would be given to the hungry wolves to be torn to pieces. That was the law concerning sacrilege against the trees of the gods.

Some of the Frisians had been to Rome, the Eternal City, and had there learned, from the cruel Romans, how to build great enclosures, not of stone but of wood. Here, on holidays, they gave their prisoners of war to the wild beasts, for the amusement of thousands of the people. The Frisians could get no lions or tigers, for these fierce brutes live in hot countries; but they sent hundreds of hunters into the woods for many miles around. These bold fellows drove the deer, bears, wolves, and the aurochs within an ever narrowing circle towards the pits. Into these, dug deep in the ground and covered with branches and leaves, the animals fell down and were hauled out with ropes. The deer were kept for their meat, but the bears and wolves were shut up, in pens, facing the great enclosure. When maddened with hunger, these ravenous beasts of prey were to be let loose on the Christian Danes. Several aurochs, made furious by being goaded with pointed sticks, or pricked by spears, were to rush out and trample the poor victims to death.

The heart of the beautiful Fos-te-dí-na, who had heard the songs of the singer of faith in the one God and love for his creatures, was deeply touched. She resolved to set the captives free. Being a king's daughter, she was brave as a man. So, at midnight, calling a trusty maid-servant, she, with a horn lantern, went out secretly to the prison pen. She unbolted the door, and, in the name of their God and hers, she bade the prisoners return to their native land.

How the wolves in their pen did roar, when, on the night breeze, they sniffed the presence of a newcomer! They hoped for food, but got none.

The next morning, when the crowd assembled, but found that they were to be cheated of their bloody sport, they raged and howled. Coming to the king, they demanded his daughter's punishment. The pagan priests declared that the gods had been insulted, and that their anger would fall on the whole tribe, because of the injury done to their sacred tree. The hunters swore they would invade the Danes' land and burn all their churches.

Fos-te-dí-na was summoned before the council of the priests, who were to decide on the punishment due her. Being a king's daughter, they could not put her to death by throwing her to the wolves.

Even as the white-bearded high priest spoke, the beautiful girl heard the fierce creatures howling, until her blood curdled, but she was brave and would not recant.

In vain they threatened the maiden, and invoked the wrath of the gods upon her. Bravely she declared that she would suffer, as her Lord did, rather than deny him.

"So be it," cried the high priest. "Your own words are your sentence. You shall wear a crown of thorns."

Fos-te-di'-na was dismissed. Then the old men sat long, in brooding over what should be done. They feared the gods, but were afraid, also, to provoke their ruler to wrath. They finally decided that the maiden's life should be spared, but that for a whole day, from sunrise to sunset, she should stand in the market-place, with a crown of sharp thorns pressed down hard upon her head. The crowd should be allowed to revile her for being a Christian and none be punished; but no vile language was to be allowed, or stones or sticks were to be thrown at her.

Fos-te-di'-na refused to beg for mercy and bravely faced the ordeal. She dressed herself in white garments, made from the does and fawns--free creatures of the forest--and unbound her golden tresses. Then she walked with a firm step to the centre of the market-place.

"Bring the thorn-crown for the blasphemer of Fos-i-té," cried the high priest.

This given to him, the king's daughter kneeled, and the angry old man, his eyes blazing like fire, pressed the sharp thorns slowly, down and hard, upon the maiden's brow. Quickly the red blood trickled down over her golden hair and face. Then in long, narrow lines of red, the drops fell, until the crimson stains were seen over the back, front, and sides of her white garments.

But without wincing, the brave girl stood up, and all day long, while the crowd howled, in honor of their gods, and rough fellows jeered at her, Fos-te-dí-na was silent and patient, like her Great Example. Inwardly, she prayed the Father of all to pardon and forgive. There were not a few who pitied the bleeding maiden wearing the cruel crown, that drew the blood that stained her shining hair and once white clothing.

Years passed by and a great change came over land and people. The very scars on Fos-te-dí-na's forehead softened the hearts of the people. Thousands of them heard the words of the good missionaries. Churches arose, on which was seen the shining cross. Idols were abolished and the trees, once sacred to the old gods, were cut down. Meadows, rich with cows, smiled where wolves had roamed. The changes, even in ten years, were like those in a fairy tale. Best of all, a Christian prince from the south, grandson of Charlemagne, fell in love with Fos-te-dí-na, now queen of the country. He sought her hand, and won her heart, and the date for the marriage was fixed. It was a great day for Free Frisia. The wedding was to be in a new church, built on the very spot where Fos-te-dí-na had stood, in pain and sorrow, when the crown of thorns was pressed upon her brow.

On that morning, a bevy of pretty maidens, all dressed in white, came in procession to the palace. One of them bore in her hands a golden crown, with plates coming down over the forehead and temples. It was made in such a way that, like a helmet, it completely covered and concealed the scars of the sovereign lady. So Fos-te-dí-na was married, with the golden helmet on her head. "But which," asked some, "was the more glorious, her long tresses, floating down her back, or the shining crown above it?" Few could be sure in making answer.

Instead of a choir singing hymns, the harper, who had once played in the king's hall, now an older man, had been summoned, with his harp, to sing in solo. In joyous spirits, he rendered into the sweet Frisian tongue, two tributes in song to the crowned and glorified Lord of all.

One praised the young guest at the wedding at Cana, Friend of man, who turned water into wine; the other, "The Great Captain of our Salvation," who, in full manly strength, suffered, thorn-crowned, for us all.

Then the solemn silence, that followed the song, was broken by the bride's coming out of the church. Though by herself alone, without adornment, Fos-te-dí-na was a vision of beauty. Her head-covering looked so pretty, and the golden helmet was so becoming, that other maidens, also, when betrothed, wished to wear it. It became the fashion-for Christian brides, on their wedding days, to put on this glorified crown of thorns.

All the jewelers approved of the new bridal head-dress, and in time this golden ornament was worn in Friesland every day. Thus it has come to pass that the Frisian helmet, which is the glorified crown of thorns, is, in one form or another, worn even in our day. When Fos-te-dí-na's first child, a boy, was born, the happy parents named him William, which is only another word for Gild Helm. Out from this northern region, and into all the seventeen provinces of the Netherlands, the custom spread. In one way or another, one can discern, in the headdresses or costumes of the Dutch and Flemish women, the relics of ancient history.

When Her Majesty, the Dutch Queen, visits the Frisians, in the old land of the north, which her fathers held so dear, she, out of compliment to Free Frisia, wears the ancient costume, surmounted by the golden helm. Those who know the origin of the name Wilhelmina read in it the true meaning, which is,

"The Sovereign Lady of the Golden Helm."

WHEN WHEAT WORKED WOE

Many a day has the story-teller wandered along the dykes, which overlook the Zuyder Zee. Once there were fertile fields, and scores of towns, where water now covers all. Then fleets of ships sailed on the bosom of Lake Flevo, and in the river which ran into the sea. Bright and beautiful cities dotted the shores, and church bells chimed merrily for the bridal, or tolled in sympathy for the sorrowing. Many were the festal days, because of the wealth, which the ships brought from lands near and far.

But to-day the waters roll over the spot and "The Dead Cities of the Zuyder Zee" are a proverb. Yet all are not dead, in one and the same sense. Some lie far down under the waves, their very names forgotten, because of the ocean's flood, which in one night, centuries ago, rushed in to destroy. Others languished, because wealth came no longer in the ships, and the seaports dried up. And one, because of a foolish woman, instead of holding thousands of homes and people, is to-day only a village nestling behind the dykes. It holds a few hundred people and only a fragment of land remains of its once great area.

In the distant ages of ice and gravel, when the long and high glaciers of Norway poked their cold noses into Friesland, Stavoren held the shrine of Stavo, the storm-god. The people were very poor, but many pilgrims came to worship at Stavo's altars. After the new religion came into the land, wealth increased, because the ships traded with the warm lands in the south. A great city sprang up, to which the counts of Holland granted a charter, with privileges second to none. It was written that Stavoren should have "the same freedom which a free city enjoys from this side of the mountains (the Alps) to the sea."

Then there came an age of gold in Stavoren. People were so rich, that the bolts and hinges and the keys and locks of their doors were made of this precious yellow metal. In some of the houses, the parlor floor was paved with ducats from Spain.

Now in this city lived a married couple, whose wealth came from the ships. The man, a merchant, was a simple hearted and honest fellow, who worked hard and was easily pleased.

But his wife was discontented, always peevish and never satisfied with anything. Even her neighbors grew tired of her whining and complaints. They declared that on her tombstone should be carved these words:

"She wanted something else"

Now on every voyage, made by the many ships he owned, the merchant charged his captains to bring home something rare and fine, as a present to his wife. Some pretty carving or picture, a roll of silk for a dress, a lace collar, a bit of splendid tapestry, a shining jewel; or, it may be, a singing bird, a strange animal for a pet, a barrel of fruit, or a box of sweetmeats was sure to be brought. With such gifts, whether large or small, the husband hoped to please his wife.

But in this good purpose, he could never succeed. So he began to think that it was his own fault. Being only a man, he could not tell what a woman wanted. So he resolved to try his own wits and tastes, to see if he could meet his wife's desires.

One day, when one of his best captains was about to sail on a voyage to the northeast, to Dantzig, which is almost as far as Russia, he inquired of his bad-tempered vrouw what he should bring her.

"I want the best thing in the world," said she. "Now this time, do bring it to me."

The merchant was now very happy. He told the captain to seek out and bring back what he himself might think was the best thing on earth; but to make sure, he must buy a cargo of wheat.

The skipper went on board, hoisted anchor and set sail. Using his man's wits, he also decided that wheat, which makes bread, was the very thing to be desired. In talking to his mates and sailors, they agreed with him. Thus, all the men, in this matter, were of one mind, and the captain dreamed only of jolly times when on shore. On other voyages, when he had hunted around for curiosities to please the wife of the boss, he had many and anxious thoughts; but now, he was care-free.

In Dantzig, all the ship's men had a good time, for the captain made "goed koop" (a fine bargain). Then the vessel, richly loaded with grain, turned its prow homeward. Arriving at Stavoren, the skipper reported to the merchant, to tell him of much money made, of a sound cargo obtained, of safe arrival, and, above all, plenty of what would please his wife; for what on earth could be more valuable than wheat, which makes bread, the staff of life?

At lunch time, when the merchant came home, his wife wanted to know what made him look so joyful. Had he made "goed koop" that day?

Usually, at meal time, this quiet man hardly spoke two words an hour. To tell the truth, he sometimes irritated his wife because of his silence, but to-day he was voluble.

The man of wealth answered, "I have a joyful surprise for you. I cannot tell you now. You must come with me and see."

After lunch, he took his wife on board the ship, giving a wink of his eye to the skipper, who nodded to the sailors, and then the stout fellows opened the hatches. There, loaded to the very deck, was the precious grain. The merchant looked up, expecting to see and hear his wife clap her hands with joy.

But the greedy woman turned her back on him, and flew into a rage.

"Throw it all overboard, into the water," she screamed. "You wretch, you have deceived me."

The husband tried to calm her and explain that it was his thought to get wheat, as the world's best gift, hoping thus to please her.

At that moment, some hungry beggars standing on the wharf, heard the lady's loud voice, and falling on their knees cried to her:

"Please, madame, give us some of this wheat; we are starving."

"Yes, lady, and there are many poor in Stavoren, in spite of all its gold," said the captain. "Why not divide this wheat among the needy, if you are greatly disappointed? You will win praise for yourself. In the name of God, forgive my boldness, and do as I ask. Then, on the next voyage, I shall sail as far as China and will get you anything you ask!"

But the angry woman would listen to no one. She stayed on the ship, urging on the sailors, with their shovels, until every kernel was cast overboard.

"Never again will I try to please you," said her husband. "The hungry will curse you, and you may yet suffer for food, because of this wilful waste, which will make woful want. Even you will suffer."

She listened at first in silence, and then put her fingers in her ears to hear no more. Proud of her riches, with her voice in a high key, she shouted, "I ever want? What folly to say so! I am too rich." Then, to show her contempt for such words, she slipped off a ring from her finger and threw it into the waters of the harbor. Her husband almost died of grief and shame, when he saw that it was her wedding ring, which she had cast overboard.

"Hear you all! When that ring comes back to me, I shall be hungry and not before," said she, loud enough to be heard on ship, wharf, and street. Gathering up her skirts, she stepped upon the gangway, tripping to the shore, and past the poor people, who looked at her in mingled hate and fear. Then haughtily, she strode to her costly mansion.

Now to celebrate the expected new triumph and to show off her wealth and luxury, with the numerous curiosities brought her from many lands, the proud lady had already invited a score of guests. When they were all seated, the first course of soup was served in silver dishes, which every one admired. As the fish was about to be brought in, to be eaten off golden plates, the butler begged the lady's permission to bring in first, from the chief cook, something rare and wonderful, that he had found in the mouth of the fish, which was waiting, already garnished, on the big dish. Not dreaming what it might be, the hostess clapped her hands in glee, saying to those at the table:

"Perhaps now, at last, I shall get what I have long waited for--the best thing in the world."

"We shall all hope so," the guests responded in chorus.

But when the chief cook came into the banquet hall, and, bowing low, held before his mistress a golden salver, with a finger ring on it, the proud lady turned pale.

It was the very ring which, in her anger, she had tossed overboard the day before. To add to her shame, she saw from the look of horror on their faces, that the guests had recognized the fact that it was her wedding token.

This was only the beginning of troubles. That night, her husband died of grief and vexation. The next day, the warehouses, stored with valuable merchandise of all sorts, were burned to the ground.

Before her husband had been decently buried, a great tempest blew down from the north, and news came that four of his ships had been wrecked. Their sailors hardly escaped with their lives, and both they and their families in Stavoren were now clamoring for bread.

Even when she put on her weeds of grief, these did not protect the widow from her late husband's creditors. She had to sell her house and all that was in it, to satisfy them and pay her debts. She had even to pawn her ring to the Lombards, the goldsmiths of the town, to buy money for bread.

Now that she was poor, none of the former rich folks, who had come to her grand dinners, would look at her. She had even to beg her bread on the streets; for who wanted to help the woman who wasted wheat? She was glad to go to the cow stalls, and eat what the cattle left. Before the year ended, she was found dead in a stable, in rags and starvation. Thus her miserable life ended. Without a funeral, but borne on a bier, by two men, she was buried at the expense of the city, in the potter's field.

But even this was not the end of the fruits of her wickedness, for the evil she did lived after her. It was found that, from some mysterious cause, a sand bar was forming in the river. This prevented the ships from coming up to the docks. With its trade stopped, the city grew poorer every day. What was the matter?

By and by, at low tide, some fishermen saw a green field under the surface of the harbor. It was not a garden of seaweed, for instead of leaves whirling with the tide, there were stalks that stood up high. The wheat had sprouted and taken root. In another month the tops of these stalks were visible above the water. But in such soil as sand, the wheat had reverted to its wild state. It was good for nothing, but only did harm.

For, while producing no grain for food, it held together the sand, which rolled down the river and had come all the way from the Alps to the ocean. Of old, this went out to sea and kept the harbor scoured clean, so that the ships came clear up to the wharves. Then, on many a morning, a wealthy merchant, whose house was close to the docks, looked out of his window to find the prows, of his richly laden ships, poked almost into his bedroom, and he liked it. Venturesome boys even climbed from their cots down the bowsprits, on to the deck of their fathers' vessels. Of such sons, the fathers were proud, knowing that they would make brave sailors and navigate spice ships from the Indies. It was because of her brave mariners, that Stavoren had gained her glory and greatness, being famed in all the land.

But now, within so short a time, the city's renown and wealth had faded like a dream. By degrees, the population diminished, commerce became a memory, and ships a curiosity. The people, that were left, had to eat rye and barley bread, instead of wheat. Floods ruined the farmers and washed away large parts of the town, so that dykes had to be built to save what was left.

More terrible than all, the ocean waves rolled in and wiped out cities, towns, and farms, sinking churches, convents, monasteries, warehouses, wharves, and docks, in one common ruin, hidden far down below.

To this day the worthless wheat patch, that spoiled Stavoren, is called "Vrouwen Zand," or the Lady's Sand. Instead of being the staff of life, as Nature intended, the wheat, because of a power of evil greater than that of a thousand wicked fairies, became the menace of death to ruin a rich city.

No wonder the Dutch have a proverb, which might be thus translated:

> "Peevishness perverts wheat into weeds
> But a sweet temper turns a field into gold."

WHY THE STORK LOVES HOLLAND

Above all countries in Europe, this bird, wise in the head and long in the legs, loves Holland. Flying all the way from Africa, the stork is at home among dykes and windmills.

Storks are seen by the thousands in Holland and Friesland. Sometimes they strut in the streets, not in the least frightened or disturbed. They make their nests among the tiles and chimneys, on the red roofs of the houses, and they rear their young even on the church towers.

If a man sets an old cart wheel flat on a tree-top, the storks accept this, as an invitation to come and stay. At once they proceed, first of all, to arrange their toilet, after their long flight. They do this, even before they build their nest. You can see them, by the hour, preening their feathers and combing their plumage, with their long bills. Then, as solemnly as a boss mason, they set about gathering sticks and hay for their house. They never seem to be in a hurry.

A stork lays on a bit of wood, and then goes at his toilet again, looking around to see that other folks are busy. Year after year, a pair of storks will use the same nest, rebuilding, or repairing it, each spring time. The stork is a steady citizen and does not like to change. Once treated well in one place, by the landlord, Mr. and Mrs. Stork keep the same apartments and watch over the family cradle inside the house, to see that it is always occupied by a baby. The return of the stork is, in Holland, a household celebration.

Out in the fields, Mr. Stork is happy indeed, for Holland is the paradise of frogs; so the gentleman of the red legs finds plenty to eat. He takes his time for going to dinner, and rarely rushes for quick lunch. After business hours in the morning, he lays his long beak among his thick breast feathers, until it is quite hidden. Then, perched up in the air on one long leg, like a stilt, he takes a nap, often for hours.

With the other leg crossed, he seems to be resting on the figure four (4).

Towards evening he shakes out his wings, flaps them once or twice, and takes a walk, but he is never in haste. Beginning his hunt, he soon has enough frogs, mice, grubs, worms or insects to make a good meal. It is because this bird feels so much at home, in town and country, making part of the landscape, that we so associate together Holland and the stork, as we usually do.

The Dutch proverb pictures the scene, which is so common. "In the same field, the cow eats grass; the grayhound hunts the hare; and the stork helps himself to the frogs." Indeed, if it were not for the stork, Holland would, like old Egypt, in the time of Moses, be overrun with frogs.

The Dutch call the stork by the sweet name "Ooijevaar," or the treasure-bringer. Every spring time, the boys and girls, fathers and mothers, shout welcome to the white bird from Egypt.

"What do you bring me?" is their question or thought.

If the bird deserts its old home on their roof, the family is in grief, thinking it has lost its luck; but if Daddy Stork, with Mrs. Stork's approval, chooses a new place for their nest, there is more rejoicing in that house, than if money had been found. "Where there are nestlings on the roof, there will be babies in the house," is what the Dutch say; for both are welcome.

To tell why the stork loves Holland, we must go back to the Africa of a million years ago. Then, we shall ask the Dutch fairies how they succeeded in making the new land, in the west, so popular in the stork world. For what reason did the wise birds emigrate to the cold country a thousand miles away? They were so regular and punctual, that a great prophet wrote:

"Yea, the stork in the heaven knoweth her appointed times."

Ages ago, there were camels and caravans in Africa, but there was no Holland, for the land was still under the waves. In India, also, the stork was an old bird, that waded in the pools and kept the frogs from croaking in terms of the multiplication table. Sometimes the stork population increased too fast and some went hungry for food; for, the proverb tells us that a stork "died while waiting for the ocean to dry, hoping to get a supply of dried fish."

When on the coast of the North Sea, the Land of a Million Islands was made, the frog emigrants were there first. They poured in so fast, that it seemed a question as to who should own the country-frogs or men. Some were very big, as if ambitious to be bulls. They croaked so loud, that they drowned out the fairy music, and made the night hideous with their noises. The snakes spoiled the country for the little birds, while the toads seemed to think that the salt ocean had been kept out, and the land made, especially for them.

The Dutch fairies were disgusted at the way these reptiles behaved, for they could not enjoy themselves, as in the old days. If they went to dance in the meadow, on moonlight nights, they always found a big bullfrog sitting in their ring, mocking them with its bellowing. So when they heard about the storks in Africa, and what hearty appetites they had, for the various wrigglers, crawlers, jumpers and splashers in the waters, they resolved to invite them, in a body, to Holland.

The Dutch fairies knew nothing of the habits of the bird and scarcely imagined how such a creature might look, but they heard many pleasant things about the stork's good character. The wise bird had an excellent reputation, not only for being kind to its young, but also for attending to the wants of its parents, when they were old. It was even said that in some countries the stork was the symbol for filial piety.

So the fairies of all the Netherlands despatched a delegation to Egypt and a congress of storks was called to consider this invitation to go west. Messengers were at once sent to all the red-legged birds, among the bulrushes of the Nile, or that lived on the roofs of the temples, or that perched on the pyramids, or dwelt on the top of old columns, or that stood in rows along the eaves of the town houses. The town birds gained their living by acting as street cleaners, but the river birds made their meals chiefly on fish, frogs, and mice.

The invitation was discussed in stork meeting, and it was unanimously accepted; except by some old grannies and grandpops that feared in the strange land they would not be well fed. On a second motion, it was agreed that only the strongest birds should attempt the flight. Those afraid, or too weak to go, must stay behind and attend to the old folks. Such a rattle of mandibles was never heard in Egypt before, as when this stork meeting adjourned.

Now when storks travel, they go in flocks. Thousands of them left Egypt together. High in the air, with their broad wings spread and their long legs stretched out behind them, they covered Europe in a few hours. Then they scattered all over the marshy lands of the new country. It was agreed that each pair was to find its own home. When the cold autumn should come, they were to assemble again for flight to Egypt.

It was a new sight for the fairies, the frogs and the men, to look over the landscape and see these snow white strangers. They were so pretty to look at, while promenading over the meadows, wading in the ponds and ditches, or standing silently by the river banks. Soon, however, these foreign birds were very unpopular in bullfrog land, and as for the snakes, they thought that Holland would be ruined by these hungry strangers. On the other hand, it was good news, in fairy-land, that all fairies could dance safely on their meadow rings, for the bullfrogs were now afraid to venture in the grass, lest they should be gobbled up, for the frogs could not hide from the storks. The new birds could poke their big bills so far into the mud-holes, that no frog, or snake, big or little, was safe. The stork's red legs were so long, and the birds could wade in such deep water, that hundreds of frogs were soon eaten up, and there were many widows and orphans in the ponds and puddles.

When the fairies got more acquainted with their new guests, and saw how they behaved, they nearly died of laughing. They were not surprised at their diet, or eating habits, but they soon discovered that the storks were not song birds. Instead of having voices, they seemed to talk to each other by clattering their long jaws, or snapping their mandibles together. Their snowy plumage--all being white but their wing feathers--was admired, was envied, and their long bright colored legs were a wonder. At first the fairies thought their guests wore red stockings and they thought how heavy must be the laundry work on wash days; for in Holland, everything must be clean.

Of all creatures on earth, as the fairies thought, the funniest was seen when Mr. Stork was in love. To attract and please his lady love, he made the most grotesque gestures. He would leap up from the ground and move with a hop, skip, and jump. Then he spread out his wings, as if to hug his beloved. Then he danced around her, as if he were filled with wine. All the time he made the best music he knew how, by clattering his mandibles together. He intended this performance for a sort of love ditty, or serenade. The whole program was more amusing than anything that an ape, goat, or donkey could get up. How the fairies did laugh!

Yet the fairies were very grateful to the storks for ridding their meadows of so much vermin. How these delicate looking, snow white and graceful creatures could put so many snails, snakes, tadpoles, and toads into their stomachs and turn them into snow white feathers, wonderful wings and long legs, as red as a rose, was a mystery to them. It seemed more wonderful than anything which they could do, but as fairies have no stomachs and do not eat, this whole matter of digestion was a mystery to them.

Besides the terror and gloom in the frog world, every reptile winced and squirmed, when he heard of this new enemy. All crawlers, creepers, and jumpers had so long imagined that the land was theirs and had been made solely for their benefit! Nor did they know how to conquer the storks. The frog daddies could do nothing, and the frog mothers were every moment afraid to let either the tadpoles or froggies go out of their sight. They worried lest they should see their babies caught up in a pair of long, bony jaws, as sharp as scissors, there to wriggle and crow, until their darlings disappeared within the monster.

One anecdote of the many that were long told in the old Dutch frog ponds was this: showing into what clangers curiosity may lead youngsters. We put it in quotation marks to show that it was told as a true story, and not printed in a book, or made up.

"A tadpole often teased its froggy mother to let it go and see a red pole, of which it had heard from a traveller. Mrs. Frog would not at first let her son go, but promised that as soon as the tadpole lost his tail, and his flippers had turned into fore legs, and his hind quarters had properly sprouted, so that he could hop out of danger, he might then venture on his travels. She warned him, however, not to go too near to that curious red pole, of which he had heard. Nobody as yet found out just what this red thing, standing in the water, was; but danger was suspected by old heads, and all little froggies were warned to be careful and keep away. In reality, the red stick was the leg of a stork, sound asleep, for it was taking its usual afternoon nap. The frogs on the bank, and those in the pool that held their noses above water, to get their breath, had never before seen anything like this red stilt, or its cross pole; for no bird of this sort had ever before flown into their neighborhood. They never suspected that it was a stork, with its legs shaped like the figure four (4). Indeed, they knew nothing of its long bill, that could open and shut like a trap, catching a frog or snake, and swallowing it in a moment.

"Unfortunately for this uneducated young frog, that had never travelled from home, it now went too near the red pole, and, to show how brave it was, rubbed its nose against the queer thing. Suddenly the horrible creature, that had only been asleep, woke up and snapped its jaws. In a moment, a wriggling froggy disappeared from sight into the stomach of a monster, that had two red legs, instead of one. At the sight of such gluttony, there was an awful splash, for a whole row of frogs had jumped from the bank into the pool. After this, it was evident that Holland was not to belong entirely to the frogs."

As for the human beings, they were so happy over the war with the vermin and the victory of the storks, that they made this bird their pride and joy. They heaped honors upon the stork as the savior of their country. They placed boxes on the roofs of their houses for these birds to nest in. All the old cart wheels in the land were hunted up. They sawed off the willow trees a few feet above the ground, and set the wheels in flat, which the storks used as their parlors and dressing rooms.

As for the knights, they placed the figure of the stork on their shields, banners, and coats of arms, while citizens made this bird prominent on their city seals. The capital of the country, The Hague, was dedicated to this bird, and, for all time, a pond was dug within the city limits, where storks were fed and cared for at the public expense. Even to-day, many a good story, illustrating the tender affection of The Hague storks for their young, is told and enjoyed as an example to Dutch mothers to be the best in the world.

Out in the country at large, in any of the eleven provinces, whenever they drained a swamp, or pumped out a pond to make a village, it was not looked upon as a part of Holland, unless there were storks. Even in the new wild places they planted stakes on the pumped out dry land, called polders. On the top of these sticks were laid as invitations for the stork families to come and live with the people. Along the roads they stuck posts for storks' nests. It became a custom with farmers, when the storks came back, to kill the fatted calf, or lamb, and leave the refuse meat out in the fields for a feast to these bird visitors. A score of Dutch proverbs exist, all of them complimentary to the bird that loves babies and cradles.

Last of all, the Dutch children, even in the reign of Queen Wilhelmina, made letter carriers of their friends the treasure-bringers. Tying tiny slips of paper to their red legs, they sent messages, in autumn, to the boys and girls in the old land of the sphinx and pyramids, of Moses, and the children of Israel. In the spring time, the children's return messages were received in the country which bids eternal welcome to the bird named the Bringer of Blessings.

This is why the storks love Holland.